KEYS AND CATASTROPHES

A MIRA MICHAELS MYSTERY

JULIA KOTY

BUSSTOP PRESS

First paperback edition April 2021

Cover design by Kim Thurlow
Book design by Natasha Sass

ISBN 978-1-939309-23-5 (paperback)
ISBN 978-1-939309-04-4 (large print paperback)
ISBN 978-1-939309-02-0 (ebook)
www.JuliaKoty.com

To my children Ana and Ryan,
and to my husband Joe, who still believes

ALSO BY JULIA KOTY

1

The Sunday morning light warmed the inside of the car as I turned off the highway onto the exit ramp. The long road trip was about to come to an end. A worn wooden sign with flecking white paint announced that we were in Pleasant Pond, Pennsylvania, the town I planned to call home. At least for the time being.

"Meow." Arnold wanted my attention again. *May I remind you that I did not willingly agree to this whole experiment.*

Curls of hair fell out of my ponytail. I tugged on the elastic and ran my fingers through it quickly. Juggling the steering wheel, I pulled my hair away from my face and up into a tighter ponytail. I took a deep breath.

Again, against my better judgment, I answered him. "We've already talked about this. I understand you don't want to move to a new house."

The next meow sounded more like a rumble in his throat. *I miss Darla.*

"I get it that you love Darla, but she micromanages my life. I really don't want to talk about it anymore."

Arnold's thoughts were in my mind, as clear as if he were talking to me. I had given up trying to ignore it. Because as much as I didn't want to be anything like my psychic sister, communicating with my cat had its upsides. Like company on this long car ride or reminding him to use the litterbox and not the inside of the carrier when he got mad at me.

And I'd like to remind you that I am completely over riding in this locked box.

"You have to stay in the carrier because they have rules about animals in cars."

He circled inside his carrier. *Whoever made that rule was obviously not a cat.*

"It's for your own safety." I had another mile to go before we would be on the outskirts of town.

Can we take a break?

"Not right now. I can stop up ahead and give you more treats. Let me focus on driving and not panicking, okay? Aren't you supposed to provide emotional support?"

I am not required in any way to be an emotional support animal.

"I get it, buddy. You are king. I am your human. Now let me drive."

I felt like a lunatic when I talked to Arnold. But I had spent too many months ignoring his voice in my head. It made life simpler to just listen and respond. It definitely helped with all the territorial peeing and scratching. Not me —the cat.

After the last big blow-up with my sister, I found a list of "Best Places to Live in America" and closed my eyes and poked a finger at the computer screen. I chose Pleasant Pond, Pennsylvania. I figured a town with such a name would be a great place to start a new life. After that I searched the real estate pages. That's when I saw it. This gorgeous Victorian on the cheap. Like very cheap. Of course, there was a catch, I thought, *there is always a catch.*

I was adventurous, but I wasn't dumb. Three months ago, when my money was still safely in the bank and not in the hands of my no-good ex, I flew down and checked out the place before I bought it. When I saw it for the first time, I had been pleasantly surprised. It was a tall somewhat narrow Victorian with all the eye-catching extras. It reminded me of fairy tales and secrets. Truth be told, it needed work. But not as much as I had expected. As soon as I walked through the door, I had the feeling that Arnold and I needed to be there.

The realtor, Rebecca Branson, seemed edgy throughout the house tour. When we got back to her office and settled in at her desk, I asked. "So, why is it so cheap?" I didn't mention that cheap was a relative term. Rebecca, with her manicured beach-vacation-blue nails and perfectly styled hair wouldn't look me in the eyes.

Obviously prepared for the question, she recited her response. "The town owns the house and wants to see the main street revitalized. Because this house has some issues, they've dropped the price to make it more appealing to buyers who are interested in fixer-uppers."

I nodded. I'd seen it before. Cities, but usually large cities, offering up townhomes for a dollar with the stipulation that a certain amount of money was to be put into rejuvenating the residence. Only this contract didn't require me to put any money into the place. The house was just cheap. Which was also the only reason I bought it.

After purchasing the house and thanks to my very ex-boyfriend, I only had a tiny bit left over to start the process of flipping the house, and that was assuming I ate Ramen and learned how to plant a vegetable garden.

I gave her a questioning glance.

She leaned closer. "I'm not supposed to tell you, but you might as well know. The place is haunted."

A laugh burst out of my mouth. The absurdity of it all hit me like a water balloon. Of course, it was haunted, because the universe thought it was one big joke that I could never get away from the legacy of my family. The realtor probably assumed I was laughing for other reasons. Disbelief maybe. Still, I laughed.

But she didn't even grin. Instead, she frowned at the unsigned paperwork.

"The town wants the house sold." She shoved the paperwork back in its manila folder. "I shouldn't have said anything."

"It won't keep me from buying it." My sister was the one who dealt with ghosts, not me. "I don't believe in ghosts," I lied.

She tucked a lock of her blond hair behind her ear. "You still want to go through with the sale?"

"I need to start somewhere." Now I would have a house with its own history, its own story. This was not exactly what I was looking for, but it would have to do.

She shrugged. "Okay." She pulled the paperwork back out of its folder and cautiously pushed it across the desk to me. She watched me sign *Mira Michaels* and her whole body visibly relaxed. "I used to think the same thing until I started working in that house."

Curiosity had me. "Really?"

Her body involuntarily shivered. She slipped the done deal back into its folder. "I'm happy to have it off my list, finally."

4

"Wow. That bad?" My stomach tightened. *What had I just done?* But the thought passed quickly. I had to get out from under my sister's thumb. Whatever happened, I would deal with it.

She nodded slightly and caught herself. "Goodness, now you don't want it."

"On the contrary."

"Well, then, welcome to Pleasant Pond, and please, call me Becca."

I gathered up my copies of the papers, shook her hand, and left. I was getting away from my family and proving to myself I could be an adult on my own, my sister didn't need to mother me. Haunted house or no.

Now I had returned with all my worldly possessions and Arnold crammed into my ancient Buick. Its peeling paint would fit right in with the exterior of my future home. The fact that I had sunk every last penny I owned into the house was not an exaggeration and the reality of it made me short of breath. I could live a few months on the money still in my bank account, but I would definitely need a job. The realization of it all, that I was on my own, sink or swim, hit me.

My heart pounded. My vision blurred. I pulled off to the side of the road and parked the car.

Breathe in, breathe out.

I had to prove to myself and my sister that I didn't need her constant input in my life to survive.

Arnold meowed from the carrier. "Sorry, buddy. I just needed a breather." Arnold was the one cat that didn't puke when in the car. He didn't enjoy car rides, but he wasn't hyperventilating either. That was me. Breathe in, breathe out.

What if I couldn't make the money I needed? Worse,

what if I somehow managed to do all the work and pay for it and couldn't find a buyer? Well, I would figure it out. One step at a time. That's all I could do. I wished Arnold *was* an emotional support cat. I could use some words of comfort in my head right now.

My car shook as someone drove by at a speed quite a bit more than the recommended speed limit. I glanced in my rearview but only saw the dust the car stirred up, and police lights. It wasn't until the police officer knocked on my window that I realized he wasn't pulling over the speeder that just flew by, but me.

Really? My heart rate tripled. If I got a ticket, whatever money I had would be gone. Why was he pulling me over?

I rolled down my window. The officer wore plainclothes.

"Is there a problem officer?" I was still in the middle of something resembling a panic attack and my breathing came in hitched and uncomfortable breaths.

He peered in and cleared his throat. "I pulled you over because one of your taillights is out."

Of course, he was good looking because that's what happens when you swear off all men. "Correction, I pulled myself over because I was having a panic attack. And you're not helping." My anger at the universe now got heaped on to this guy.

He examined me closer. "Do you need assistance? Are you okay?"

"What kind of question is that? Of course, I'm okay." I was not having a panic attack, I refused. I was handling this move just fine. Lying to myself came in quite handy at the moment.

"If you need assistance, I can have an EMT out here."

"How bad do I look?" I glared at him. I put my hand up.

"Don't answer that." I hadn't slept well in two days and I had a feeling it showed on my face.

"If you don't need any assistance, you are free to go. But get that taillight fixed." He rested his hand on the open frame of the window, tapped it twice and stood back.

"Why are you giving me grief? Why don't you pull that speeder over instead of giving a girl a bigger panic attack for arriving in town?"

He paused for a moment. "Sorry, about that. I'm Detective Lockheart. Welcome to Pleasant Pond." His eyes looked me over, again. "Are you sure you're okay to drive?"

"I'm fine." I snapped.

A frown creased his face. "Get the taillight fixed." He turned and strode back to his car.

A deep breath in didn't calm me down. I closed my eyes. When I opened them my rearview showed the police car still sitting there. I took another breath. I hoped this guy didn't work in this town, but knowing my luck...

"We best get going huh, Arnold?"

His lack of response meant he was more than done with this little journey of ours. I just hoped he'd be okay with the change. Maybe this old house will have lots of mice for him to chase.

I put the car in drive and pulled back onto the road. I amended my thought—I'd rather have ghosts than mice.

WE CONTINUED our adventure into our new town. I drove down Main Street per the stated twenty miles per hour speed limit. I certainly could not afford a ticket.

The town center was compact and small. The bank and post office shared a low, squat tan brick building. The grocery store looked more like a house on the corner. Almost every other storefront was dark and empty with "For Lease" signs in the windows. At the end of the street stood a brightly painted diner called Soup and Scoop. My stomach growled. The clock in the dash read 11:30. I wasn't meeting Rebecca until 12:30 when she'd hand me the keys and do a final welcome walk-through. There was still time for a bite. I pulled into the small lot in back of the Soup and Scoop.

"Sorry Arnie. I'll be quick, I promise."

A low rumble from the carrier.

"I know, I know. I swear I'll let you out as soon as we get to our new home, you'll love it."

Hopefully, the Soup and Scoop had cat-friendly policies and they would let me bring him inside. If not I'd have to rely on take-out. Although, the idea of me handling soup in the car or at the new house without furniture was not something I could see happening without some drama.

I dropped a couple of Arnold's favorite treats into his carrier. His black nose turned away and he licked the long ebony colored fur on the underside of his paw. If anything, Arnold kept his fur as neat as Hercule Poirot's mustache.

I grabbed his carrier and walked around to the front of the diner. In direct contrast to the storefronts along Main Street, which looked empty and vacant, the diner's exterior was a chic combination of sky blue and teal with shining chrome accents. The bell on the door rang as I pushed it open and walked into the diner's wonderfully ethereal yet comforting vibe. The light blue sparkled Formica tables, white checkered floor, and additional chrome accents made me feel instantly welcome.

I stood there with the cat carrier, not daring to step further in with a cat in hand. Of course, Arnold picked this moment to be completely silent and not help me get the attention of the waitress at the back of the room. Her dark blond hair was pulled up in a ponytail and she wore a classic 50's diner apron. But she must have heard the bell because she turned to us and waved for me to wait. She finished the order for a cute guy with dark hair and short beard. He was the only one in the place and I sincerely hoped he lived in town. For him I'd give up my thoughts of avoiding relationships. The waitress came over, smiling.

"Hi there, how can I help you?" Her ponytail bobbed.

"Table for one?" I looked down at the floor by the door. "Can I bring my cat in here? I didn't want to leave him in the car."

"I totally understand. You can take him to your booth with you."

"Really?"

"I own the place. And my brother is the only one here now. I don't think he'll mind." She waved a welcoming hand toward the booth near the door.

Arnold meowed. I decided it best not to translate my hyper-privileged cat's response.

"Thanks. I appreciate it. Arnold appreciates it too." I gave the carrier a slight nudge to remind him of his manners.

She crouched down to peer into the carrier, her gray eyes bright and cheerful. "Hey there, little guy, I bet you're ready to get out of that box." She stood and pulled out a menu from behind the napkin dispenser. "Here you go, and if you have any questions just let me know. I'll be at the counter making a shake."

"Will do." I hoped the food was good because if it were, I could see myself here often. Then I checked reality and realized I had very little, if any, expendable cash to splurge on eating out.

I pushed Arnold's carrier into the booth so it faced me,

even though he would clearly let me know if he needed anything. "It's okay, buddy, I'll make this fast—I promise."

He settled his head on his paws to wait it out. *Be quick about it.* Patience wasn't his strong suit.

The blue vinyl booth was cozy; the Formica table with its chrome trim was adorable. Reading the menu, I grinned. Soups, sandwiches, and ice cream.

The soup of the day was handwritten on the menu—squash bisque—which sounded perfect. It even came in a bread bowl. Awesome. I opted for a milkshake, chocolate malt. Soon after I put the menu on the table, the waitress came back with a glass of water, a cloth napkin, and silverware. "What can I get you?"

"The squash bisque sounds great, and can I have that in a bread bowl?"

"Gluten-free or regular?"

"You have gluten-free here?" In a small town I didn't think they would have gluten-free anything.

"I'm gluten-free myself. I feel like the gluten weighs me down, spiritually."

The spirituality thing reminded me of my sister, but I couldn't help but like this woman's bubbly personality. "Just the regular, and can I get a chocolate malted milkshake?"

"Of course, you can. Oat milk or regular?"

"Regular whole milk."

She smiled just as happily and took my order. "Are you making your way up to the Grand Canyon?"

I wasn't sure what she meant. "Isn't that in Arizona?"

She grinned. "The Pennsylvania Grand Canyon. It's nearby. People stop here on their way out to visit it."

I had never heard of the Pennsylvania Grand Canyon. "Sounds like a great place to visit."

"It is." She wrote everything down on a small

chalkboard. "I'll have Robbie put this right in for you. We don't want your kitty to have to wait too long."

Because this day has already been insufferably long. Arnold grumbled.

"I'm moving in today, just up the street. So, I have cat food. He won't have to wait long at all," I reminded him.

Her eyes lit up. "That's wonderful. We'll be neighbors. I live in the next house over from the restaurant."

"That makes you my first new friend." I felt just as cheesy saying it as it sounded.

"I am Aerie, by the way." She stretched out a hand and we shook.

"My name is Mira Michaels. Nice to meet you."

"Mira, you have a wonderfully bright aura and it's very nice to meet you too."

I smiled. Yep, serves me right. I exit my relationship with my psychic sister and my first new friend runs along that same vein. Well, not the exact same, I hoped. But her infectious positivity seemed to clear the air, and I didn't mind so much.

Within minutes Aerie brought me a beautiful bread bowl of soup that smelled of sage and pumpkin squash. The bisque was the best I'd ever tasted. It had just the right amount of sweet and savory, and the bread was so fresh that I couldn't help but dip it into the soup over and over again. I focused so much on my meal I had stopped "listening" for Arnold who meowed to remind me of the real purpose of today, and it wasn't enjoying a bowl of soup.

"Sorry, buddy. I'll finish up," I whispered.

I dabbed my mouth with my napkin and folded it neatly on the table. The cloth napkins gave the restaurant such a homey feel. I asked Aerie for the check, but she interrupted me." Don't worry about it. It's on the house. Welcome to Paradise Pond!" She beamed another smile at me.

"Are you sure? I don't mind paying." I pulled out my phone.

"What are neighbors for? I hope your move goes smoothly. And I hope to see you here again."

"Thanks, Aerie."

I gathered up Arnold who shifted his weight in the carrier and meowed again. It was time to move in.

Her cute brother looked up from his burger as I was heading out the door. "See ya." He raised a hand and waved. I grinned and waved back. I hoped so.

2

My new home stood within walking distance from the Soup and Scoop, on the corner of Market Street and Main Street. I parked against the curb in front of the house. First things first, poor Arnold had to get out of the car. I grabbed the carrier and the litterbox, along with the dish for water which he said cramped his whiskers, and headed for the house.

If Becca the realtor didn't arrive soon, I could always let Arnold have run of the backyard. But I realized that might not be the best idea. A beautiful wrought iron fence surrounded the yard. The charm of it made me smile, but it certainly left space for a wily cat to sneak through. And Arnold definitely qualified as wily. Even if we argued about safety that cat would do what he wanted anyway. Rust marred the fence in a few places but nothing a good can of Rustoleum couldn't fix.

I knocked on the front door and looked up at the house. It was tall and narrower than a modern house and stood very stately on the corner of two roads, its sidewalks hemming it in. The black shutters weren't merely decorative but could be closed against oncoming storms. I knocked again and turned the door handle. It opened, so Becca must be here.

I pushed the door and stepped inside. "Becca?" I shouted. "I need to put Arnold in the bathroom so he can have some food and his litter box." I made my way through the foyer and dining room, down the hall toward the stairs. The powder room occupied the space under the stairs and was simple with only a toilet and a small sink. An adorable little bathroom. I opened it up, stepped inside, and closed the door.

"Here you go, buddy." I opened his carrier. Arnold shot out like a rocket. I set the shallow cardboard box that held the litter nearby and he made a break for it.

Privacy. Please.

I stepped back into the hall for the count of thirty and opened the door.

I didn't need to have a psychic bloodline to know that Arnold was relieved. I praised him as the good little kitty-boy that he was and poured him a bowl of water. "I'll be right back with your food."

The quaint cracked tile of the powder room floor reminded me of the history of this house and, unless the floor had a problem, I'd avoid changing it. The tight space didn't leave much room, so I pushed the carrier into the corner next to the toilet. Arnold might want to rest, cozy on the towel in there.

Cozy. You're kidding right?

"Yes, yes, I know cozy is the last word you'd use to describe it." I highly doubted that for any reason Arnold would relax inside the carrier after the long ride we had from Massachusetts.

I had to get his food from the car. "Becca?" I shouted

again. Maybe she had walked here and was outside. I arrived back at the car and grabbed the bag of food, but instead of going into the house I walked around the side gate to the backyard. The house itself had magnificent peaked roofs and eaves, but it was also the fenced-in backyard with the little matching shed in the far corner of the yard that had sold me.

It even had a small terraced gardening plot right outside the kitchen door. I thought about how cool it would be to pick my vegetables or herbs and head back inside to cook dinner. But I shook my head and reminded myself of the plan. *Flip it and sell it. I am a rolling stone*, I reminded myself.

A huge pine tree grew in the center of the yard. The ground under it lay bare but, in my imagination, it would be beautifully landscaped with a pebble base outlined in river rocks. I would even add a bench or a swing.

My eyes followed the height of the tree to its top, and across the blue sky to the roof of the house, admiring the beauty of the brass lightning rod with its north, east, south, west, cross pole and its tarnished grasshopper sitting at the top. I wasn't sure how to get that thing down to polish it, but it would happen.

As I walked to the side of the yard, something crashed on the sidewalk behind me. I spun around as a second gray slate shattered near the concrete steps. I took a deep breath. My heart raced; just another thing that had to get fixed on the house. Finding someone to lay new slate on the roof might be a problem. That was one thing I was sure that I couldn't do on my own.

I leaned against the fence and looked out onto Main Street and down to the right where the Soup and Scoop stood. Anytime I didn't want to cook, there it was. That soup had been darn good. I pretended I didn't have to worry about money right now.

I glanced up at the house again. As soon as I got the keys and did the walk-through with Becca, this place was mine. There were a number of necessities that had to happen before I went to bed tonight. I had to turn on the water and the electricity and check the water heater. I'd like to know if I was going to have a hot shower tonight, after moving everything into the house. I took a deep breath and headed to the kitchen door to see if it was open. I shouldn't have been surprised that it was unlocked, this being a small town and all. But I personally would be locking all my doors, regardless. Old habit. Safety first. The door was a 1970's addition. I'd probably swap it out to make it more in line with the original date of the house. If and when I could afford it.

The panes of glass were fogged, and I could barely see inside. As I stepped across the threshold, something bulky lay on the floor in the kitchen. My first thought was: *Who left a pile of clothes in my house?* But when I strode around the door and stood inside the kitchen, realization hit.

It wasn't a pile of clothes; it was a body.

FOR THE SECOND TIME TODAY, I couldn't breathe. It wasn't just any body on the floor—it was Becca's body. And Becca was clearly dead. She lay there, her eyes staring unseeing, a broken chair leg next to her. The sight of blood on the side of the piece of wood swept a wave of dizzying nausea over me. I stepped back into the yard. Fresh air. I sat, put my head down, and tried to catch my breath.

How many times had my sister done this? Arrived at a

murder scene and done her thing? When I felt like I could breathe enough to speak, I pulled my phone out of my back pocket and dialed 911.

The sirens woke me out of a daze. I didn't actually remember making the call. Obviously, I had told the dispatcher, a woman—I remembered now—there was a body in my house. In my kitchen. It was Rebecca my realtor. Oh, poor Becca.

A heavy-set officer with a tight crew cut walked across the yard toward me.

"Afternoon," he greeted me. The sun glinted off the small metal crest on the front of his hat and I couldn't take my eyes from it. Everything felt like a dream. A nightmare. One that I hoped I could wake from. But waking didn't seem to be in the cards.

"I'm police chief Orsa. Where's the body?"

I pointed weakly behind me and through the still-open kitchen door. I couldn't go back into that room.

The police chief was back before I knew it. And suddenly everything felt real. There's a dead body in my kitchen.

"I'll need to take your statement on what happened here today." The police chief walked around to stand in front of me again. His uniform was neatly pressed and buttoned tightly over his stomach.

I nodded. I told him what I knew: Yes, I had gone into the house, my cat was inside. No, I hadn't touched the body. No, I wasn't here when it happened. No, I hadn't seen anyone else around. Oh, and no, I hadn't killed my realtor.

Then, Aerie, the waitress, hurried toward me. "Chief Orsa, she's innocent."

"The investigation will prove that, or not, Ms. McIntyre."

He stepped back into the kitchen. His footsteps echoed as he walked around the room.

"She ate lunch in the diner at eleven thirty until about twelve fifteen. I can vouch for her." She dropped down next to me, hooked her arm under my limp one, and sat with me, shoulder to shoulder. Her reassurance made me feel better. I took a deep breath. "I had lunch at the Soup and Scoop," I choked out. Why couldn't I focus?

Chief Orsa came back outside and noted something on his notepad. "This location is now an active crime scene. You cannot stay here. And you cannot leave town until the investigation is complete."

Aerie put a hand on my shoulder. "That's okay, Chief, she can stay with me."

I felt so disconnected. "My cat..."

"I love cats, remember? It's going to be okay." She squeezed my arm reassuringly. I nodded and glanced back at Chief Orsa, hoping he'd lock up when he left. I tried not to feel like I had just sunk my life savings into a fixer-upper I could never sell. Like I wouldn't have to tell potential buyers that it was haunted, *and* someone was murdered in it.

Okay. So, that happened.

Time to collect my wits and get it together.

I took a deep breath and finally addressed Aerie. "I need to get Arnold out of the bathroom under the stairs."

"I can help with that." Aerie walked close beside me to the front of the house.

The front door stood open and officers were affixing crime scene tape all over the place. This was not how I envisioned the start of my fixer-upper career.

Between the two of us we managed to get Arnold back into the carrier. I had a harder time calming my mind enough to listen for his thoughts on the situation. Explanations would come later. I grabbed his dish.

"You can leave the litter. I have a cat at home. No worries." Aerie smiled at me.

"Arnold is particular. I'll bring it. He has issues with sharing." I chose not to share his affirmation of that fact.

We left my new crime scene house, put Arnold in my car, and drove back to the Soup and Scoop.

"Let me just close up the diner, then I can get you settled at my house. Okay?"

I nodded and Aerie popped back into the diner for a few moments. *Why should I share the front seat with a stranger?* Arnold complained. I ignored his territory dispute.

Aerie eased back into the car and held Arnold's carrier on her lap. "Robbie said he'd lock up for me."

We pulled up next to her house, which sat on the other side of the parking lot from the diner, a Victorian not too unlike mine. Narrower, though, and with a sidewalk between it and the house next to it.

I tried not to think too much—about anything—as I went through the process again of settling Arnold, this time in Aerie's bathroom.

What, may I ask, is going on? He gave me a death glare.

"Later," I whispered.

"Let me change the sheets in the guest bedroom." Aerie pointed me to the stairs, and as I walked up, she grabbed some sheets out of a hall closet, grabbing a pillow from the top shelf. "You're right next to the bathroom—I'm on the other side. My brother Jay's room is down at the end of the hall."

"Oh, your brother lives with you?" This new tidbit of news helped to crowd out the mantras of dead-body-in-my-new-kitchen or new-house-is-a-crime scene. I opened the door to the guest room. It was small but cute—and above the old wooden dresser was a picture of the diner with a banner, GRAND OPENING, stretched across the roof.

Aerie nodded. "Yeah, this was the house we grew up in. Our parents passed a few years ago, so we share the place."

"It's convenient that you can live together," I said. "Although I think if I lived with my brother, I'd probably want to kill him half the time." I threw a hand to my mouth. "I can't believe I just said that. I'm so sorry."

Aerie grinned sadly. "No worries, it's just a figure of speech. I suspect we'll all be a little edgy for a while." She pulled down the white comforter and we worked together to put the sheets on the bed. The room had an antique wooden rocker in the corner with a crocheted afghan hung over the top.

"We do have our moments when we get on each other's nerves, though. I mean, he's my big brother. He has learned every possible way to annoy me."

I grinned. "Family is like that."

"Is that why you moved? Sorry. I don't mean to be nosy."

"Oh, no. I mean, yeah, my sister can get on my nerves, but I moved out here to, well, to find my own way. I figured I'd flip the house, make some money, and find the next house to work on. I guess it's my latest passion."

"Are you good at flipping houses?" She tucked in the corner of the top sheet and pulled the comforter back in its place.

"Seeing as this is my first one? No." I sat down on the bed.

Aerie came around the side of the bed and gave me a hug. "Don't you worry about it. This will get cleared up and you can get back to starting your new passion." She walked around the bed and smoothed the comforter tightly against the mattress.

"I can't believe someone killed Becca." Aerie shook her head.

"I always thought small towns were meant to be safer than the city." I flopped back onto the soft bed thinking of all the crimes my sister helped solve, most of those in Boston, but quite a few in our small hometown too.

"Ours isn't this week, that's for sure." Aerie shook her head. "I just don't get why anyone would hurt Becca. Well, unless..." She stopped tugging the bed covers. "But that's just a rumor."

3

I woke the next morning sleep deprived and cranky. Not because the bed wasn't comfortable, but weird dreams plagued me all night long of dead people and cats. Maybe Arnold had been meowing in my brain in the middle of the night. I had woken up with the certainty that I had to take matters into my own hands today. No murderer would scare me out of my new house. And I wouldn't rely on some small-town police chief to solve my problems for me. The quickest way to get back into my house and new life was to solve the crime and close the investigation. After our adventure on the way down from Massachusetts, I had confidence I could do this. I didn't need my sister's help. I could solve the murder.

My sister was going to be livid. Forgetting to call her when I arrived in town was unforgivable in her eyes. She'd worry. Personally, I thought it was just a part of her controlling nature. Still, I picked up my phone. Had she left messages even though I told her not to? The phone was dead. I tossed it back on the bed. But I realized I had better charge it if I wanted to know when I could return to the house.

I stretched, put on some clothes, grabbed my toiletry kit, and headed to the bathroom. I ran my fingers through my hair and quickly brushed my teeth to make myself somewhat presentable before I headed downstairs. When I walked through the hallway, Aerie's bedroom door stood open, and her bed was made. I guessed Aerie was an early morning person. I looked at the watch still on my wrist from yesterday. Six-thirty.

The smell of coffee coming from downstairs drew me to it like a magnet. I came around the corner into the kitchen and stopped dead in my tracks. Aerie's brother, Jay, stood there in nothing but his boxers holding a steaming cup of coffee, sipping it slowly. My eyes traced his biceps. Obviously, he worked out.

He glanced up. "Hey, there. I'm Jay." A mischievous grin played on his face.

Had I been smiling? My face burned. Heat rose from my neck to my cheeks. "Nice to meet you. Coffee?" I squeaked out.

"Sure." He reached into the cabinet and pulled out a mug, which he filled to the rim and handed it to me.

I stared at it for a moment. There wasn't any room for cream or sugar. I took a long sip and tried not to grimace. "Any cream or milk?"

"Sorry, no. Aerie doesn't do dairy, and I drink mine black."

"Any sugar?"

He smiled and his dark eyes twinkled. "That, I can help you with." He reached into the cabinet. "I have a secret stash in the back." He winked.

He placed the open bag of sugar on the counter and

handed me a spoon. I put two heaping spoonfuls into my coffee and stared into my mug trying hard not to glance up at him.

"So, you bought the old Spencer house?" He sipped his coffee and took a seat at the kitchen table. "Heck of a way to get introduced to the town. Sorry about that."

I shrugged. "It sucks." I was such an idiot. What was I saying? I took a big gulp of coffee letting it burn the back of my throat and took a seat at the opposite end of the kitchen table. "Thanks for the coffee."

"The least I could do." He watched me for a moment too long, and I self-consciously stared into my coffee mug and took another slow sip. Relief washed over me when Aerie swept in through the kitchen door.

"Good morning, fellow humans! How are you all? Mira, did you sleep well?" A yoga mat tucked under her arm, she wore a tank top and yoga pants, with her hair pulled into a tan scrunchy that matched her blond hair.

"I slept. Thank you for putting me up."

"Not a problem." She propped the yoga mat in the corner of the kitchen and lit the gas under a kettle that sat on the stove top.

"You certainly couldn't sleep in that house last night." She turned to her brother. "Hey Jay, did you know that Mira is going to fix up the Spencer house. You know, flip it and sell it?"

He looked at me from across the kitchen table. "Oh, yeah?"

I tried to smile, but not in my usual nervous goofy way.

"Yeah, she is. Maybe you can help her out with the work."

Why would Aerie's brother want to help me to fix up my house? The question must have shown on my face.

"I own a construction business."

Realization hit me. "Oh." I breathed in and closed my eyes. I don't think I've ever been any dumber, in any conversation, ever.

"Jay, if you get dressed, I can take you both over to the diner and ask Robbie to make us breakfast. We're trying out the vegan scramble today." Aerie poured herself a cup of tea into a travel mug.

I must have flinched because Jay began to laugh. "Hey Air, I'm going to bet your new friend doesn't much care for fake eggs." He stood. "I've got to be at the site early today. So, I gotta run." He snickered once more. "Nice to meet you, Mira. Good luck with breakfast." He disappeared down the hallway.

"Are you up for it?"

"Sure, but let me take care of Arnold first; I bet he isn't too thrilled about being forced to stay in the bathroom all night."

"Oh, the poor boy! You can let him out. He can play with Snowball. She's shy and likes to hide, so he can have the run of the house; she won't mind."

Jay and Aerie argued over who got the shower first. Their voices echoed in the upstairs hall and it made me giggle and I felt a bit better after everything that had happened.

After feeding Arnold, he explored the house.

Why have I spent the last day and night in human litterboxes?

"There was a problem at the house."

I smelled dead human.

"Yes. Our realtor Becca was killed."

Territorial spat?

"No, humans aren't like cats."

He growled an affirmation. *Humans make absolutely no logical sense with their actions.*

"To you, a cat, they may not, but everyone's actions are made for reasons, I just need to figure out what they are."

We should contact Darla on that thing you carry in your back pocket.

"It's a phone. I'm not texting or calling Darla."

She makes sense.

"She will tell me she told me so, then she will go back to micromanaging my life. No. I'm not calling her."

She knows things.

I couldn't deny her psychic skills completely. "Not everything. I am not calling her. I can handle this. This is my life and I'm not letting this get in the way of my independence."

I hope so because I don't want to spend another night trapped in a bathroom. He stressed that last word as if I had left him in a cesspool and not a spotless tiled restroom.

Still, while I showered, I almost talked myself out of staying. What did I know about solving a murder? Tailing criminals on the highway was one thing. Darla had solved crimes before, but I wanted nothing more to do with the psychic part of my family. What could I possibly do to find a killer?

Whatever skills I did have had to work because I refused to crawl back home. And poor Becca, she deserved better. I had planned to fix up that house, sell it, and leave with the cash. That was still my plan and nothing, including a murderer, was keeping me from it.

BY THE TIME we arrived at the diner, the cook was already in the back prepping for breakfast.

"Robbie usually opens up early, about the same time I'm heading to my yoga class. I teach over at the community center." She grabbed an apron off the hook and tied it around her waist. "Smells like he's already starting the soup." She leaned toward the open bar that separated the kitchen from the dining counter. "Hey Robbie, what's the soup today?"

"Chili bean," he shouted from the back.

I peered into the kitchen. Robbie was a fit middle-aged guy who looked like he was all business. I remembered the delicious taste of the squash bisque from yesterday. "Robbie's soup is incredible."

"I couldn't run this place without him. I'm not much of a cook myself."

I stared at her. "But you own a diner?"

"It was my parent's place. Jay co-owns it too, and well, the diner kind of supplements my income from teaching yoga. The hours work well together." She finished tying the apron around her back and people started filing in for breakfast.

"Plus, I get to talk to everybody in town. Something I love to do anyway." She grinned. "You get to order first." She walked around the long counter while I climbed onto a blue upholstered stool. The soothing vibe in the diner made it easy to understand why a good part of the town would stop here each morning to start their day. "What will you have?" She put chalk to her chalkboard.

"Eggs, toast, potatoes, and coffee?" I secretly prayed she wouldn't give me the vegan option.

"Vegan?"

"Sorry. I kind of like the original."

"Don't be sorry. It's fine by me. Maybe I can get you to try some of the vegan desserts later." She winked and smiled at me and she wrote up her orders on a larger chalkboard that hung on the wall in the kitchen.

I peeked in at Robbie and was surprised to find him staring at me. His dark piercing eyes seemed to accuse me of something. And then he turned abruptly and went back to the grill.

Suddenly, I worried about the safety of my meal. I shook my head; that was silly. I was just overreacting from everything that happened. He might have heard about Becca's death and wondered if it was my fault. I couldn't have asked for a worse introduction to everyone in town.

I attempted to lighten things up by complimenting his cooking. "Hey Robbie, I really liked yesterday's squash bisque. That and the bread bowl were the best I've ever tasted."

As he leaned forward, Robbie didn't seem as threatening now. "Glad you liked it." He leaned out across the bar. "It's an old family recipe. Got it from my ma. She'd be glad to hear it."

I breathed a sigh of relief. Now I could eat without freaking out that every bite could be my last.

While waiting, I took in the atmosphere of the diner. All but two tables were full of people. Aerie looked happy chatting and taking orders from everyone. The customers appeared to know her well, asking her questions, and she, asking after their families. So, this was what small towns were like. Everyone knowing everything about everyone. I smiled slightly. I supposed everyone knowing your business could have its downsides too, but when solving a murder, it seemed like a very useful thing. The police chief from yesterday was finishing up his breakfast. Without even thinking about it I walked myself over to him just as he rose and dropped a ten-dollar bill on the table. "Ms. Michaels." He tipped his hat.

"Good morning. I'm wondering if I'll be able to get into my house today."

"No." He looked me up and down as if he were hoping to find a murder weapon on my person. "The detective will need to go through the house until he's satisfied."

"Do you know when that will be?"

"No." He pushed past me. "If you don't mind. I have work that needs to be done. You won't have the house until I say we're finished with it."

"What? You can't be serious."

"This is very serious, Ms. Michaels. We're investigating a murder." He turned and left the diner. The door jingled as it closed.

"Now what do I do?" I said out loud.

Aerie, nearby, turned. "Do you need anything?"

"My house would be nice." I sighed. "Sorry, the police chief won't give me a time that I can go back to the house."

"You and Arnold are welcome as long as you need."

"Thanks, Aerie. I'm just a little frustrated."

Robbie waved from the window.

Aerie smiled. "I think your breakfast is ready."

AFTER WHAT WAS, again, one of the best meals I'd ever eaten. My stomach hoped that Robbie wasn't the killer. I thought back to yesterday. They said people were usually killed by acquaintances, people who knew them. Ugh, what an awful thought. But that would also mean someone in town had done it. If my alibi was that I was eating lunch at the diner, then Robbie's alibi was cooking my lunch at the diner.

The uncooperative nature of the police chief and the detective did not suit me at all. I had watched my sister work on cases before, sort of. I could figure this out, I hoped.

I decided to walk around for a while and check out the town. I would make a point of heading back to my house and examine the situation for myself. The ornery police chief had my cell number. Whether he would call me when they were finished with the house remained to be seen.

I placed cash next to my plate along with a healthy tip. I didn't want Aerie to keep paying for my meals out of pity. She was already putting me up in her house. I checked my phone case, not much cash left. The bank was down the street in the same building as the post office. I should set up a post office box, too.

I was going to prove to Darla and myself that I could make it on my own without any help. I refused to let the fact that someone was murdered in my house keep me from proving I could adult on my own. I would solve this and continue with my original plan.

"Thanks, Aerie. I'll see you later, if that's okay?"

"Absolutely." She waved as I left the diner and started my walk down Main Street.

4

One of the first things I needed to do was to learn more about Becca, and if I was going to figure out who would want to kill her I'd have to learn more about the town and the people who lived here.

My walk around Pleasant Pond showed me just how compact it was. With a few empty storefronts, a grocer, and the essentials: police, fire department, post office, and bank, I could easily and quickly walk the length of the town center. But it gave me the feeling of a well-worn lounge chair, a little beat up around the edges but nonetheless cozy. I decided to head to the bank first and get some cash. Thankfully, it was a branch of the larger bank I used in the city. One less thing on my adulting to-do list. I didn't have to worry about moving money over or creating a new account. Easy enough to get the cash I needed from the ATM.

It was a beautiful cool morning and the sky was a deep blue with a few clouds skirting by. The sidewalks were uncrowded, but a few people were out, and by the looks of it, heading to the Soup and Scoop.

I glanced back toward Market Street at my house. It still

had the yellow crime scene tape wrapped around the gate, and someone's beat-up white Chevy sedan was parked outside. I let out a sigh. I would run my errands first, money and post office box, and then share a word or two with the detective who felt he needed to spend extra time monopolizing my house.

The low tan brick building that held both the post office and the bank looked like it had been built in the 1970's; a blunt contrast with the wood-framed grocer's building across the square. At least I had the option to walk to get groceries. My old Buick had barely limped into town.

ATM first. I wanted to make sure I could cover the cost for Robbie's great food, and for Aerie's tips, which she totally deserved in spades. As soon as I crossed the street, I noticed a handwritten sign taped across the front of the ATM: Out of Order.

Yeah, that's my life so far in Pleasant Pond. Out of Order. Sheesh. I pulled open the door to the bank and was pushed aside by a little old lady. She wore a clear plastic kerchief on her head and was pushing a 3-foot-tall grocery cart in front of her. She almost took my legs out from under me.

"Watch where you're going, young lady." She buzzed around me like a race car driver and headed out the door.

"I'm sorry," I said as I stepped into the foyer. She said nothing more to me but continued out the door.

"Oh, don't mind her." The young teller behind the counter waved me over. "Believe it or not she's a very nice lady most days. She's having problems right now because her son is giving her grief about money or something like that."

I raised an eyebrow at this. The bank teller probably shouldn't be sharing everybody's financial issues with the public.

She saw my look. "Oh, don't worry. Mrs. Orsa has complained to everybody in town. I'm surprised you don't already know."

"I'd like to get some cash, but the ATM..."

"Yeah. Sorry about that, we're waiting on a repair guy from the city, but they haven't given us a time frame yet on when he can come out here. But don't worry, I can help you out. Can I have your account information and your driver's license, please?"

I got out my phone and pulled my ID from its case next to the couple of bills that were left.

She looked down at my license. "Oh, so you're the one who bought the old Spencer place." She looked through dark fringed bangs and smiled.

"That's me," I said.

"Geez, were you the one that found Becca?"

She wasn't asking a question. She already knew I had been the one to find the body.

"Poor Becca. She was sweet, but I did hear that her father was back in town."

"Her father is a possible suspect?" I prodded for more details.

"Well, Mr. Branson is one of those mean drunks. Before he left town, he was always starting bar fights and getting arrested."

"People think he might have done something to Becca?"

"Everyone knows he came back to town to get money from her and that she didn't want anything to do with him."

"Do you think he did it?"

"You never know what goes on in other people's houses."

"I guess not." Ah, the rumor mill. She handed me my sixty dollars and I folded the bills and squeezed them along with my ID back into the phone case.

"Oh, and a word of caution, Mrs. Orsa comes in every morning at this time lately to complain, so if you want to avoid her, come in at 8:05 a.m. I would if I could."

"Note taken. Thanks again." I shoved my phone into my back pocket.

"Oh, I didn't introduce myself. I'm Ellie Bracken. Nice to meet you." She reached over the counter to shake my hand. I noticed she had an empty piercing at the side of her petite nose. She had multiple rings on her fingers, and a large area of her wrist was paler than the rest of her arm. Charm bracelets I bet, and my guess was she wasn't allowed to wear them at work.

"Mira Michaels, but you already know that." This was the place to come for juicy gossip. Maybe I could use that right now. "Do you know who the detective is that's working on the case? I think he's still in my house, and I'd like to talk to him."

The blue of her eyes darkened. "Oh, that's Dan." I think I heard her swoon.

"Do you know his last name?"

She snapped out of her reverie and a frown creased between her brows. "Lockheart. He's been detective for a year now."

Great. The guy that pulled me over. "Thanks, for your help Ellie."

"No problem. Hey, if you talk to Dan, can you tell him Ellie says, hi?"

"Um, sure." Mental note: Ellie has the hots for Dan the Detective man.

As I was leaving, an older man wearing a dark suit came out from the back offices. He advanced toward me with his arm out and a smile. "Welcome to town, Ms. Michaels." He took my hand and pumped it up and down. "My name is Mr.

Meyer. I'm the bank manager here in town. We're glad to have your business."

His exuberance was overwhelming.

"If there's anything we can do, we are here for you."

"Thanks." I managed to extricate my hand from his grip.

I glanced over at Ellie, who hid her face and appeared to be laughing. Now was as good a time to make my exit.

"Thanks again, Mr. Meyer. Ellie." She held back her giggles with a pinched grin.

As the bank door eased closed behind me, I heard Mr. Meyer reprimand Ellie about something, probably the giggle fit. But I would wager if anyone really wanted to know, Ellie would probably share any and all information with the next customer.

THE POST OFFICE didn't have a large foyer like the bank. The entrance opened to a simple area in front of the counter where patrons could order stamps or ship something. The town's post office boxes took up most of the left wall. Small three by five-inch boxes with little brass doors that held a small window and a lock. The elderly lady that nearly sidelined me at the bank was currently fighting with her key in a lock, trying to get it out. She had the locking mechanism engaged, so the key wouldn't come out until she turned the key another 40 degrees.

I couldn't let her struggle. "Ma'am, can I help you with that? You just need to..." I bent over to reach her post box.

"I can figure it out by myself." She yanked on the key as hard as she could, in doing so turned the key the amount it needed. Her hand flew back, she quickly pocketed the key, took out her mail, and left. Leaving the post box hanging open.

I called to her. "Ma'am, your box..." But she was already out the door.

"Oh, don't worry about it. I can close it from this side." The man at the counter ran behind the boxes and expertly reached through and pulled the door shut.

I met him back at the counter. "Hi. I'm Mira Michaels. I'm moving in, hopefully, today. I'm wondering if I can rent a post office box?"

"Name's Mike. Nice to meet you." He held out his hand for a shake.

"Hi, Mike." I shook politely.

"I can set you up with box 172. Can you fill out this form while I get the key?" He went into the office and came back with a brass key with the number on it.

I paid the deposit with my credit card, mentally reminding myself to keep track of how much I spent on the card.

"Do you want to test it out?"

"Sure. I took the key and found box 172. I was grateful that it was central in its location. My 5'3" height would mean I'd be on tippy toes for the higher boxes. The key slid in easily, I turned it to the right, and the door opened.

"Works great. Thanks, Mike." I closed my new post box.

"So, are Dan and Chief Orsa done with your house yet? I heard about poor Becca."

"I haven't gotten a call yet from Chief Orsa. Maybe I should find him at the police station and ask."

"Oh, I wouldn't do that. Just check in with Dan. He's much easier to deal with than the chief. Don't want to upset you or anything, but Chief Orsa doesn't like newcomers much."

"I was already under that impression." My previous conversation proved that point.

"I hope he's the exception and not the rule for ya."

"Thanks, Mike. I'll see you around."

"You know where to find me."

I chuckled. Mike seemed like a good guy. The chief of police, not so much. The more I thought about it, the angrier I got. Where did he get off being so rude to me? I wasn't the killer.

I decided I'd had enough waiting around. It was time to confront the elephant in the room...or the detective in my house, about when I could have it back. But I wasn't asking. I was taking my house back and that was that.

Frustrated and convinced that the police were messing with me, I marched across the street to my house. I had worked too hard to get the money I needed to start my new business and my new life. An ornery small-town chief of police who thought he could push me around wasn't going to sidetrack my life.

I understood investigating a crime scene but from the conversation I had at the diner with Chief Orsa and just now with the postmaster, I was beginning to think he was keeping the house from me just because he could.

I wanted my house back. They had been at it all day yesterday and the detective's car was still parked in front of my house. *My* house.

The detective walked out of my front door carrying a large box. He wore a white button-down dress shirt and pants, immaculately pressed for having worked on a murder scene. He was clean shaven with a deep frown on his face. His dark hair was parted on the side. This was definitely the same guy that pulled me over when I first got into town. I sighed. The detective carried the box to his car.

I gathered my courage and marched up to him. He didn't flinch.

I tossed a curl of hair out of my face. "Exactly how much longer do you expect to be here, Mr. Lockheart? This is my house."

He glanced down at his box and then he looked at the trunk of his car, took out his keys, and in a very leisurely fashion, unlocked the trunk. He slowly, *slowly*, put the box in the trunk and slammed it closed. He looked at me and swallowed. "I'm done."

"Oh?" That knocked the wind out of my sails.

"Yes."

All the frustration of the past twenty-four hours spilled out of me. "First the chief, gives me grief about when or even if I can move in, and then you take your sweet time. I certainly hope you have all the evidence by now." My hands were on my hips.

He straightened and squared his shoulders. "How would you know what evidence is, or how to go about collecting it?"

"I know what evidence is."

"Whatever books you have read, Ms. Michaels, I'm sure it's not quite the same as a real murder investigation." There was the hint of a condescending grin on his face.

I stood there, dumbstruck. How dare he. "You have no idea who I am, what books I have read, or what my background is."

"Oh? Are you a former investigator?"

"No."

"Have you recently worked as a consultant for law enforcement?"

"No." As mad as I was, I refused to mention my sister's

name or what she does. Not to mention the adventure I had on the way down.

"Then I believe our conversation is over. You may return to your house. Welcome to town." He got in his car and started its engine.

I glared at the back of Detective Lockheart's head. "Jerk," I mumbled under my breath.

ONCE I CALMED DOWN, I gathered my wits for the second time in two days. I needed to check the kitchen. It was some kind of morbid fascination, or more likely fear. But I needed to be sure I wouldn't find a body this time.

I walked away from where Detective Lockheart's car fumes left me wheezing and headed for the gate that would let me into the backyard and the kitchen door.

My hand shook as I touched the dark brass doorknob. "Oh, stop it you. Cut it out. Nothing is going to be there." The fogged window glass didn't reassure me.

Touching the knob lightly, I pushed the door open with a shove. Even though a second ago, I had been hoping the door was unlocked, I was instantly mad that the police had left without locking it. My anger propelled me into the room.

No body.

"Thank God." Without a thought I crossed myself, like I was taught as a kid.

The place reeked of disinfectant. I kept my breathing shallow. The air felt dense, so I was still afraid something was here. I took another step. "This is my house now," I reminded myself.

A glimpse of something made me swing around with my

arms raised, wishing I had finished those karate self-defense classes last year. It was only dust motes floating on the air. Just my nerves. A moment before, I could have sworn it was a ghostly outline of a woman in a dress.

"I'm a mess." I took a deep breath.

I walked around the kitchen. The place had been cleaned spotless, cleaner than I would have expected. Any possible clues as to who had killed Becca were now with the police. I tried to remember the kitchen as I saw it yesterday. What I could recall were only jumbled images of her body and the bloody chair leg. The broken chair was gone too. The police had taken it as evidence. Its twin stood against the wall. I made a mental note to donate that chair. I'd rather sit on the floor. Nothing here would help me solve this. I'd have to start asking questions. People share the most interesting things when asked.

Right now, what I needed was to set things right and get my stuff moved in. The sooner the better. "I'm not going to chicken out of this." I gave myself a pep talk as I walked through the kitchen to the dining room. "I'm here. This is my house, and I'm going to make it beautiful."

The wallpaper in the dining room was dingy with accumulated dust telling me just how long the house had stood vacant. It was decorated with a beautiful dark teal filigree motif that I liked so much I wondered if it was possible to clean this old wallpaper instead of replace it.

The hardwood floor needed little more than a good polish. I could imagine this house in its glory, and I'd make sure it was again.

Renovation was a challenge I couldn't wait to take on.

I shook myself out of the reverie. I needed to get back to Aerie and let her know she wouldn't need to put me up for another night. I was more than ready to start living in my new home.

My cell phone rang. It was my sister. I sighed. Darla always called to warn me of some terrible decision I was about to make. I dismissed the call and shoved the phone in my pocket. I knew what my decision was, and it was to solve this murder and start my home renovation with a clean slate and a killer in jail.

5

After another wonderful meal courtesy of Robbie, I helped to close the Soup and Scoop at two-thirty. Aerie explained the restaurant only served breakfast and lunch, so her workday was done. We headed back to her house.

"I don't know why you won't just stay another night. Why sleep on a cold floor when you could sleep here?"

"It's not that I don't appreciate the hospitality, Aerie, it's just that I feel like, well, I feel like I need to prove my ownership of the house or something." I couldn't seem to find the right words to voice my need to rip off the band-aid and get this all behind me.

"Are you sure? I wouldn't mind."

My heart melted. She was such a sweet and kind person. "This is something I need to do on my own."

Aerie nodded reluctantly. "Can Jay and I at least help you check the house out to make sure it's safe?"

I smiled. "Yes. You guys can check it out and make sure I'm safe." I gave her a hug. "We barely know each other, and you feel like a best friend already."

"That's a good place to start."

I didn't have much to pack. The biggest obstacle was getting Arnold back into the carrier. Twenty-four hours and he already felt at home enough to hide from me. Luckily, Aerie and Jay knew all the cat hiding places in their home. Although, I was the one to find him under what had been my bed.

"I found him!" I shouted. He dug his claws into the carpeting and would not come out. I could barely reach him. He had managed somehow to press himself into the furthest corner against the wall. "What are you up to?" I asked him.

I want to stay. My senses are telling me to stay.

"We can't. We need to go to our own home," I whispered.

No.

Aerie ran down the hall and into the room. I stopped trying to talk Arnold out of hiding.

When Aerie saw where he was, she cleared her throat and yelled, "Jay! Can you come up here? We need your arms."

Jay got down on the floor next to me to assess the situation. He smelled like soap and cut pine. This made me break out in a nervous sweat. I definitely could not afford to be attracted to him, I reminded myself, again. Rolling stone, that's me. Not sticking around. No ties, no commitments, no worries. I had done the whole settle-down-with-a-boyfriend thing, and it had blown up in my face. That relationship imploding was half the reason I was in this town.

Jay stood back up. "I'll move the bed away from the wall and you guys can snag him."

I closed the bedroom door to eliminate that avenue of escape. Aerie crouched on one side of the bed, and I crouched on the other.

Jay lifted the bed away from the wall. I had to admit that I was caught staring at his biceps instead of watching for Arnold who bolted right past me and onto the windowsill. He howled. His golden eyes darted at me in angry accusation.

"I guess he really likes it here." I nervously giggled.

Aerie walked over to Arnold. With a concerned look on her face, she petted him, and he calmed. She took a step toward me. "Maybe you should stay tonight?"

Jay put down the bed. "Air, let her go if she wants to go."

She turned to argue. "It's just that... Well, okay." She picked up the cat carrier and held it open for me while I plucked Arnold off the sill. Surprisingly, he went right inside without wily cat antics.

"I'll call if I have any problems at the house."

"We're still going to walk through with you to make sure it's safe and locked," Aerie said.

"Sometimes, Air, you can be too much." Jay shook his head but smiled.

"Well, sometimes I need to be too much, so you'll listen to me." She punched him playfully on the shoulder.

I packed Arnold up in the car and watched as Jay and Aerie climbed into his gray pickup and then followed me the two blocks to my house. I shook my head. They were being silly. But secretly I was glad they would be there when I opened the door again. I guessed the afternoon visit hadn't dismissed all of my anxiety over the place.

WHEN WE ARRIVED at the house, I turned on all the lights, which for this place meant only the overhead lights in a few of the rooms. I had Arnold in one arm and his dish in another. I figured while we moved things from my car into the house that the safest place for him right now would again be the powder room under the stairs.

"Sorry, buddy."

He meowed low in his throat. *Again?*

"I swear it's only for a little bit." Sometimes that cat...

Once Arnold was confined to the bathroom, Aerie opened her bag and pulled out a stub of tied up dried plants and a butane lighter.

"What's that?"

"This is sage. It's a great purifier of spaces. I'd like to purify your house. Would you mind?"

"Um, I don't mind. You can do all the purifying you want."

Once she lit the sage, they smoldered. The scent reminded me of roast chicken. Better than the antiseptic musty old-house smell that surrounded us.

Jay didn't seem to mind moving things in while Aerie walked through the house room by room chanting and waving smoke around.

I held the door for him, and he'd hold the door for me while we unloaded everything from the car into the empty dining room in relative silence.

At this point, Aerie came down from upstairs. "I've purified everything...even the attic, which is huge, by the way."

I realized I hadn't actually been in the attic yet. Something to explore later.

"We should check the windows and doors, and make sure everything is locked up tight." Jay started with the kitchen which still gave me the chills.

I made my way into the living room at the front of the house and checked that window and the one on the side of the house that faced main street. I met Aerie in the hall near the stairs. "While I was up there, I checked the windows. All locked."

"Okay. Looks like I'm good, you guys. I still can't thank you enough for everything."

"Not a problem." Jay waved Aerie over. "Let's let Mira settle into her new home."

Aerie reluctantly nodded. She bounced over and gave me a hug. "If you need anything, just call, okay? I'm right down the street."

"Absolutely. No problem." I was a little nervous, but I needed to do this solo—well, me and Arnold.

We finished our goodbyes and I promised to see them at breakfast tomorrow morning, early.

After closing the front door and locking it I headed straight for the bathroom to let Arnold out. "Hey pal, good news, it's all yours."

He said nothing but immediately sniffed everything and tentatively walked the perimeter of every room in the house.

I found him in the upstairs bathroom lapping up some dripping water in the tub. "I guess I'll need to check on YouTube to learn how to fix that."

Or, I thought, better to talk to Jay about fixing it. Sigh.

I walked through all the rooms and then decided to set up my bedroom in the room next to the bathroom, instead of the master bedroom. Maybe because the only things I had were a camping cot and a suitcase, which looked much smaller in the master bedroom than in here. Everything smelled of sage which surprisingly left a cozy feel. I'd have to thank Aerie again for that as well.

Arnold purred and rubbed my leg before I got into bed.

I will keep watch.

"You don't need to keep watch; everything is locked up."

I scratched the fur between his ears and under his chin. "You're a good kitty."

I know.

He let me pet him for a bit more then walked over to my pillow and curled up into a fluffy ball. But he kept his ears perked.

After reading for a lot longer than I should have, I fell asleep with Arnold lying next to my head like a cozy warm hat.

I DREAMED of smoky rooms and meowing cats, which then shifted into me sitting on a stone bench in an open area across from a dark-haired man whose face I didn't recognize. I felt like I knew him. He smiled and reached out his hand and I shook it happily. "I'm Arnold, it's so nice to meet you," he said, and, as we shook, his hand morphed into a delicate paw that I knew very well. Arnold my cat now sat where the man had been.

"Nice to meet you too." I understood why I had recognized the man. Happily, I went on with our conversation. "You're a wonderful pet-friend."

"Thank you. You are an acceptable cat-person. I especially like the new wet food you bought while we were on the road."

"I'll remember that when I wake up." I totally understood that I was dreaming and having a conversation with my Arnold who used to be a person... and I didn't think anything about this was odd in any way.

Suddenly, Arnold's face changed from peaceful charm to startled concern. "We need to leave." He reached across to my face and patted my cheek.

Confused, I wasn't sure what was going on.

"Now." I felt his claws on my face.

I woke to find Arnold with claws outstretched, prodding my cheek. He began to howl. The feeling of hands at my back pushing me up out of bed forced me to sit up.

I shook the last of the sleepiness from my mind and listened intently. I didn't hear anything, but then the space between Arnold's howls was pretty short. I scooped him up and stood. He squeezed out of my grasp and bolted through the door in the direction of the stairs. I followed him, not sure what was going on. The house was silent. I didn't smell anything. Yet with the combination of the dream and Arnold's urgency, I followed him to the front door. He jumped and scratched until I opened it. We stumbled outside.

Just then a woosh of hot air radiated from the house. A muffled bang came from behind us. The air itself seemed to push me away. I tripped over the sidewalk into the street. I looked around for Arnold and saw him near the gate.

My mind tried to figure out what was happening, but even in my half-asleep fog, I understood that Arnold had just saved my life. I picked him up and cradled him. "Thanks, buddy. I don't know how you knew, but thanks."

I nuzzled the fur around his neck, and he purred back. A crackling sound from the back of the house jolted me fully awake and I ran to the backyard. Nothing was going to ruin my house. Not a murder or explosion, or fire, or whatever Arnold had just saved me from. I took two strides before I was grabbed from behind.

"Are you okay?"

I spun around; it was Jay.

I tried to catch my breath. "Oh, my goodness, you scared the crap out of me."

"Sorry. Stay here, though." He jogged in the same direction I had been heading. "It sounds like fire."

"What?" I ran behind him to see an orange glow around the back of the house. In a millisecond I envisioned everything I owned burned to a cinder on the ground. I charged into the backyard.

Jay grabbed a large clay pot, dumped out the poor dead plant, and filled it with water from the outside spigot on the side of the house.

Flames leapt out that stupid 1970's kitchen door as Jay doused it with water. When he came back to fill it again, he reached into his pocket. "Stay back. Here." He tossed me his cell phone. "Call 911."

For the second time in two days, I made the call. Even as the dispatcher informed me they were on the way, I heard the sirens blaring down the street.

Helplessly, I watched Jay battle the flames with water from a pot that had a hole in the bottom. I turned to find Arnold.

Another plus of living in a small town—I thought, wrestling Arnold into my car so he was safe—it doesn't take long for the first responders to arrive.

6
_____

Once the firemen had things under control, Jay took back his phone and called Aerie to drive Arnold and me back to their house. We waited for her on my front lawn, bathed in the red lights from the firetruck. I didn't know what time it was, but it was likely very, very early in the morning. Jay alternated between asking me if I was okay and telling me everything would be fine. But there was nothing okay or fine about standing in the middle of my front yard in my pajamas watching the side of my house burn down. The firemen wouldn't let me back inside to get anything, so when Aerie arrived, I grabbed Arnold out of my car and held him close.

The thought of rebuilding something as expensive as a kitchen had me in the grips of a full-on panic attack as we sat in Aerie's kitchen where she tried to talk me down.

"Take a deep breath in. Fill your lungs, feel your back expand. Now slowly exhale and let your shoulders drop."

That actually helped. I could feel my shoulders relax. I hadn't realized they were practically in my ears.

"Breathe in, expand. Open your heart center." She kept

her eyes on me the entire time. Like I might explode at any moment. "Exhale, relax your shoulders."

Aerie must be a great yoga instructor. My body totally relaxed as I listened to her soothing voice.

"Now keep breathing slowly. Close your eyes and simply be."

I did as she instructed. My body relaxed, but my mind wandered, and soon I was thinking about what happened right before the explosion. The odd dream where Arnold tapped my cheek and when I awoke to him howling. The urgency to follow him, the feeling of being pushed as I ran from the house.

I breathed slowly in and out and watched it all unfold again and again. Something nagged at me. Had I heard something, or seen something? What was I missing?

I remember being hyper-focused on watching Arnold head for the front door. Had I glanced at the kitchen? Thinking through it a fourth time and paying attention to my memory of us nearing the front door, I realized I had heard a sound. But I couldn't place the sound at all. I had no idea what it was or what it meant.

I had a feeling deep down that this fire was connected to Becca's murder and if someone wanted to light a fire under me to find them, they certainly hadn't scared me away.

Then the reality of the night came back, along with the glaring fact I had barely any money, supplies, or know-how to fix that big huge burned out hole in the back of my house.

I abruptly laughed out loud. The sound startled me, and I opened my eyes to see it surprised Aerie as well.

"Sorry." I looked over at her apologetically. "I thought about how absurd, that of all the things that blew up, it was my kitchen."

"You can eat at the diner free of charge for as long as you

need to. We'll give you soup to go for dinner—doesn't that sound awesome?" Aerie offered. "Personally, I wouldn't miss this kitchen. I think Jay cooks more than I do. I mostly use the tea kettle and the fridge."

Robbie's soup for dinner every night would certainly help. But I couldn't just live off the kindness of my new friends. "Maybe I'll cook up something for us to eat. Cooking is something I actually follow the directions for, as opposed to everything else I do. Obviously, I can't follow real-life directions at all."

"Don't say that."

"I feel stupid. I bought a house that almost killed me. My sister was right. I'm too impulsive, I don't look at all the facts first. I get too emotional about my decisions, and don't look both ways before crossing the street." I legitimately sat there and pouted.

"Stop beating yourself up. We don't even know if the gas line is faulty in the house."

"Well, yeah, the person that inspects your house before you buy it...that's who is going to find that stuff before you move in." I had told Rebecca I'd have an inspector in to do this, but his schedule got busy and I wanted to hurry up and buy, so I went ahead with the purchase of the house. "I am so stupid."

"Okay, enough of this negativity. It's time you tried some of my famous desserts. Well, Robbie makes them."

"They're vegan, aren't they?" I groaned.

Aerie grinned slightly like she was up to something. "Yep. I brought some home."

"Do I have to eat them?" I attempted to joke.

"Trust me." She picked up a glass storage container and brought it to the table.

After my second piece of chocolaty almond tort, with Aerie smiling next to me, I felt a bit better.

"You know you can stay with us. Jay won't mind, he's out of the house most of the time at work.

"Thanks. If it's not too much to ask." A mental picture of the gaping hole in the side of my house popped into my head and I fought back the urge to cry.

"Mira, you are the first fun thing that has happened in this town since high school."

"Since I came to town there has been a murder and a house explosion."

"See! Excitement." Aerie was being kind, but there was a sparkle in her eye.

"Not the kind of excitement I like. That's for sure."

"Oh, I don't mind it at all." She stood up and stretched.

"Aerie, you're a little weird."

"Yes. Jay likes to remind me." She yawned.

As if on cue he walked in the front door.

He was wet. His t-shirt clung to his chest and he was covered in soot. "Dan just kicked me off the site," he grumbled. Then he turned to me and handed me my cell phone. "You okay?"

"Thanks for getting this for me. I'm fine." And I actually felt better. Whatever it took, I would stay on track. Murders, fires, I'd figure it out. "You really didn't have to stay over there, Jay." A dark smear trailed across his right cheek like eye black on a football player and I tried not to sigh like a teenager.

"Yes, I did. I needed to see what they found. I don't think it was electrical or gas, those looked like they were updated in the 70's or 80's."

Aerie jumped in. "You think someone set the fire? See Mira, I told you it wasn't your fault."

"You can stop being so excited about this," I told her.

"When I got there the side window of the kitchen was open. Did you open it before you went to bed?" Jay asked.

"No, I didn't touch anything after you both left."

Jay nodded, his lips in a grim line. "I told Dan I didn't think you would open the window and he told me he was running the investigation and that I was invited to leave. So, I left." He pointed toward the bathroom. "I need to clean up, Air, do you mind?"

"Go ahead. You own this place too." She shook her head. "I don't know why he always defers to me when it comes to the house. Sheesh."

"So, someone wants to kill me now, too?" I had to laugh, or I would cry. The whole situation was absurd. My sister would get the biggest I-told-you-so out of this. I refused, absolutely, positively, to call her and give her that opportunity.

Jay came back out of the bathroom with cleaner hands and slightly less black under his eye. "I've got an early job tomorrow. I'm going to bed." He turned and started up the stairs.

"We'll be right behind you." Aerie took my plate and wiped down the counter.

I stood. "I can help you with that."

"I'm so accustomed to doing it at the diner, it's second nature." She scooped the crumbs from the table. "What if you come in to work with me tomorrow?"

"You don't have to keep feeding me." I did have *some* money.

She shook her head. "No, it's not that. I mean, of course you can have your meals there. The Soup and Scoop is a place where everyone comes to talk and to find out the news."

I understood what she was getting at. "You mean I might be able to listen in, like an undercover investigation?"

"It wouldn't surprise me if we learned something about what is going on." She closed the container of cake and put it in the refrigerator.

"If there's one thing I'm going to do, it's to find out who did this. Would you mind?"

"Not at all. The only thing you have to do is keep me updated."

"Deal."

"Let's get to bed. It'll be an early day tomorrow. Hey, do you want to come to my yoga class in the morning?"

"Sure. Wait. What time is it?"

"Class starts at six. But we don't have to leave the house until 5:45. It's a short walk to the community center."

I checked my watch. It was already past one o'clock. Time to power nap. And hope I didn't have any more dreams that led to me evacuating the house.

Arnold seemed to understand. He purred while he rubbed against my leg. "Come on buddy, time for a cat nap."

THE NEXT MORNING came a whole lot faster than I wanted it to. Aerie offered me a glass of lemon water in place of a cup of coffee. "You won't want the caffeine in your system before class. It'll affect your level of relaxation."

I yawned and rubbed the sleep from my eyes. "Waking up this early is affecting my level of relaxation."

"Come on. I promise this will be good for you."

The weather was sunny if still a bit cool. The community center was located on Elm Street which was just past my house on Market. As we walked by, I noticed Detective Lockheart's car parked in front. Early riser.

Aerie nodded at the car. "Hopefully, this means he'll be finished soon, and Jay can help you clean up."

I didn't even want to think what cleaning up meant. "Let's get to yoga. I need a dose of that relaxation." I picked up the pace and walked faster, away from the house. Aerie understood and changed the subject.

"I think you'll really like this class. It's one of my favorites. Vinyasa yoga is very calming."

"I could definitely use calming at this precise point in my life, Aerie." The idea of twisting myself up into knots though, did not sound relaxing.

"Vinyasa yoga deals with movement and the breath."

"So, all I have to do is breathe?"

"And move. But I'll show you how to do everything. It's easy, I promise."

The community center was a squat brick building that stood next to a tall Catholic Church with a plaque outside stating the date it was built. Aerie pulled out a key, unlocked the door, and propped it open. She slid out a sandwich board sign and placed it out front. The lettering read, Yoga Classes This Morning.

"Come on in and we'll find you a yoga mat. I need to turn on the heat and set up the music."

Aerie walked through her morning ritual to prep for class. She turned on an aromatherapy diffuser and placed her mat in the center with a nearby speaker for the music. The building appeared to be built in the 1980s instead of the 1880s like the church. The community room was spacious and in the back was a closet where I helped Aerie pull out a handful of yoga mats to make them available for her students.

"Go ahead and lay out your mat. I'll be right here at the front, but I'll walk around the room too."

"Would you mind if I stayed in the back?"

"If that's where you feel comfortable then that's where you should be."

"Thanks, Aerie. Especially for doing everything for me lately. I really appreciate it."

"Your level of gratitude is inspiring. It's one of the best ways to get through life."

People began to arrive for the class, laying out their mats in an orderly fashion and chatting with each other. They introduced themselves to me and I quickly forgot everybody's name. A whole lot of good that would do me if I was going to figure out the mystery of the murder and fire at my house. I did recognize Ellie from the bank. She waved to me and settled down just as Aerie started class. The crabby old lady was even here. Aerie had more power than I thought if she could get that woman to relax.

"Good morning," Aerie greeted everyone.

"We'd like to welcome Mira to our class today. This is her first Vinyasa yoga session."

I gave a awkward wave and felt my face heat up with embarrassment.

"All right, everyone, arms raised. Breathe in and breathe out as you fold forward."

I raised my arms and tried to fold myself in half. Tried. And when Aerie said, "Let's just hang here for a little bit," I groaned.

The woman next to me giggled under her breath. I was glad I was making an impression on everyone in my yoga class. After lots of breathing in and breathing out, raising my arms up and down and doing a number of push-ups, planks, and twists, the class was almost over, and I was a sweating mess.

"Everyone, lie on your back for savasana." I had no idea

what that was, but I lay on my back and watched out of the corner of my eye.

"Breathe in, close your eyes, and breathe out. Focus on your breath. And feel your body melt into the floor."

I listened to Aerie's soothing voice as she talked us into a deeper level of relaxation. I could feel myself melting into the floor. And then in my mind's eye I saw a woman in a dress shaking her finger at me. *It's in the kitchen.*

"What?" I sat bolt upright.

My shout startled everyone out of their relaxing trance.

"Sorry," I whispered.

"Okay, I guess that's all for today." Aerie gave me a questioning look. "I'll see you all tomorrow morning for another great Vinyasa flow."

I stared at the floor as I rolled up my mat. Aerie walked over. "Are you okay?"

"I'm really sorry." I hustled myself over to the closet and returned my mat.

"It's fine, but are you sure you're okay?"

I could see her concern. "I guess I got super relaxed and didn't realize I was still in class." Even I knew this was a lame excuse. But I was not about to tell her that I thought a ghost was talking to me.

7

O n our walk back to Aerie's house I didn't speak. I was too preoccupied forcing myself to forget about the ghost and how badly I embarrassed myself by shouting at the end of a quiet yoga class.

I utterly refused to get sucked into my sister's messed-up world. No way. And why did it have to follow me here? I was 445 miles from my past. Why here and now? Couldn't I just start over? The last thing I needed or wanted was to be more like my sister. Let's take stock... Murder. Arson. Ghost in a dress.

While Aerie showered, I stood in her kitchen sipping coffee that Jay was kind enough to leave in the coffee maker. Thinking about him brewing the coffee made me think about his hands, specifically the hand that grabbed me before I rushed into danger in my backyard. Why had he been outside my house in the middle of the night? But he certainly didn't mean me harm—he had tried to protect me. Hadn't he?

I pondered who would want me dead...and why. I focused on the why because no one here knew who I was.

Or did they? Wait a minute, were there people here who knew that my sister was famous? That would change things.

I stifled a yawn as Aerie came down the stairs.

"Still sleepy?" She had pulled her hair back in her usual work ponytail.

"Maybe if I learn something today, I can sleep better."

"I hope I can help with that. Are you ready to witness the behind-the-scenes at the diner?"

I grinned. Aerie's excitement at showing me her restaurant proved to me just how much she loved the place.

Aerie handed me an apron. "You can help by bringing out the dishes as Robbie plates them." She ran through the table numbers and I did my best to memorize them.

Robbie was already frying bacon for the morning rush and it smelled fabulous. While Aerie set the tables, I sneaked into the kitchen to find out what he knew.

"Is that real bacon or the other stuff?" My stomach growled loudly.

Without looking up, Robbie replied, "It's real." He flipped six pieces at a time with the spatula. "Want a piece?" He grinned.

"Sure," I told him. "How long have you been working here?"

"A while. Aerie's mom hired me years ago. Right before she...well, you know."

I didn't know. But I nodded. I figured that was for Aerie to share. Robbie handed me the piece of bacon on a saucer with a fork he pulled from above the stove.

"Thanks." The salty thin bacon practically melted in my mouth.

"I've got orders." Aerie cheerfully appeared in the kitchen and transferred the orders to a chalkboard on the side of the wall near the stove.

I glanced into the dining area and was surprised to see it full. "Wow. That was fast. Sorry, I'll come out and help."

"No worries, it's more helpful if you bring the plates when they are ready. Plus, the diners aren't in a rush. Most people are here for the gossip." She finished writing up the orders. "They've all heard about the fire last night. Hard not to with the sirens. Come on out and we'll show them that you're not burned to a crisp. We can even mention your hero cat's role in the rescue." Aerie pushed me out into the waiting crowd. "See folks, she's fine. Not sure how keen she is to be staying in town, so I suggest we all make her feel welcome."

"What?" I gaped at her. We needed to have a talk about my introvert tendencies and how I didn't like to be the center of attention.

Aerie winked.

I got a few offers for breakfast, a cup of coffee and lots of questions. I nodded and smiled at everyone. Thankfully, Robbie called up the orders and I ran back to the kitchen window to hide.

Robbie rattled off table numbers and I handed out the plates table by table. Each plate of breakfast, from the beautifully scrambled eggs to the gorgeous stacks of pancakes, made me appreciate his skill as a diner chef. Surprisingly, I received all of the admiration as I handed out each plate. Every time I stopped at a table, I was questioned by those waiting for their orders. My best chance at getting information anyone might have about the fire or what happened to Becca was now.

I got more than I bargained for. Everyone in town had a theory that the house—my house—was cursed or haunted. Which led to dead people.

I wanted to inform them that houses didn't kill people.

But that wasn't as much fun to them as discussing the past owners and their oddities. Or making guesses on why the house sat empty for so long and the noises people heard coming from it.

The most interesting rumor I heard was that Becca's father had been seen in town. And most were quick to talk about the abusive alcoholic that he had become to his children after his wife had died. But no one could link him to a possible arsonist that would attempt to burn down my house. Spontaneous combustion came up once, and that's when I stopped asking questions and focused on serving the meals.

That is, until a familiar, albeit irritating, face showed up. Dan the detective sat down at the counter and ordered his breakfast and coffee. Robbie cursed under his breath when he noticed Dan placing his order.

As I brought him his plate, I asked him how long it would take him this time to finish his detective work and whether he had found anything.

"Look, I get it that your boyfriend, Jay, is worried about you. I do. But I've got enough issues with this investigation. He can't go walking around the crime scene touching everything, he's contaminated whatever evidence might be there."

"Jay? He's not my boyfriend."

"He seems overly involved." He glanced at his watch. "I'm late and I have work to do. Can I have the check, please?"

Who did Detective Lockheart think he was to assume Jay was my boyfriend? My face flushed just thinking about it. I went to the computer and printed out his stupid check. But by the time I got back he had already left a ten and was heading for the door. He didn't even look back.

I picked up the ten-dollar bill and went back to the computer to cash out the check. Well, at least Dan the detective was a decent tipper. I stuffed the change into the tip jar near the register.

In the lull before lunch. I chatted with Robbie as I brought in the dishes.

"Would you like me to put these in the dishwasher?" I was amazed at the amount of work.

"No. Usually Aerie runs the dishes after the breakfast rush. But it's usually not this busy." He mumbled his last words and turned back to the grill to focus on scraping and cleaning it.

The lunch rush was not as big as breakfast but kept us busy enough that idle chatting was at a minimum. Which was too bad because I wanted to get Robbie to talk, especially as to why he had such a reaction earlier when detective Lockheart arrived.

By the end of the lunch rush I was exhausted. But that didn't keep me from thoroughly enjoying Robbie's version of the Thanksgiving dinner sandwich. Toasted whole wheat with cranberry spread, a helping of roast turkey, slices of bacon and some crispy fried onions. My jeans felt a bit tight by the time I ate the last bite. But I found enough room to pack in a piece of the vegan pumpkin pie which was remarkably tasty.

We locked up the diner at 2:45 and I turned toward my house. Dan's car was again parked out front. I wondered when I'd ever get my house back. If there was one thing I learned at the diner it was that this town had secrets, and most of them revolved around my Victorian house.

Aerie must've noticed my slumped shoulders. "Tomorrow's another day. And Jay already said he would help you with the cleanup."

There was a thought that cheered me a bit. Alone with Jay. For most of the morning if not all day cleaning up the mess that had become my house.

I headed back to Aerie and Jay's house more determined than ever to find the answers.

THE NEXT MORNING, after yoga, I phoned Detective Lockheart to ask about my house. He informed me, in a very curt way, that I was free to go back inside my extreme fixer-upper. Jay and I loaded our coffee into to-go mugs and walked over to my house. As expected, the detective's car was no longer parked out front.

"He's done," I told Jay, "but he would like us not to blow up anything that might possibly be evidence. I don't think I appreciate his sense of humor."

"He's just messing with you—he's actually a nice guy. If he hasn't found what he's looking for yet, he's not going to." Jay had a casualness about him that made it easy to talk to him.

"Are you sure you're okay helping me with this? You don't have to, you know." I didn't want him to feel obligated just because Aerie had taken me under her wing.

"I have a break in my schedule today, so it actually works out. We can get as much done today as we need to and then I can get some estimates for you on repairs." He had a shovel propped over his shoulder. His dark green t-shirt that stretched nicely across his chest read, Go Wildcats.

I laughed. "So, you're drumming up business." I tucked my hair behind my ear.

"No. Not at all." He grinned.

"I see how you work. Blow up the new girl's house and then help her rebuild it."

He frowned at that and strode ahead opening the gate.

I pulled my hair back into a ponytail. If blowing up the kitchen meant I would hang out with this guy for the duration of repairs, I'd be okay with that.

When I came around the corner and saw the devastation my heart sank. A low moan escaped my lips. The entire side of the house was black with soot. The kitchen roof had collapsed in on itself. The windows were broken, although the one at the front of the kitchen had been opened, obviously how the arsonist got inside.

"It's actually not that bad," he said.

I stared at him. "This isn't bad? The kitchen is completely gone." I threw up my arms.

"Look at it this way, now you get to create your own kitchen. A kitchen to your liking. Anything you want."

"Right now, I would settle for functional," I grumbled.

On the bright side, if there was one, I hadn't unpacked any of my meager kitchen supplies.

I put on the work gloves that Jay gave me and shook open the industrial trash bag and we picked through the rubble. I held the bag open for Jay while he shoveled in pieces of glass and burnt wood.

"This doesn't have to be depressing. Think of it as a new beginning. I can and will help you rebuild this kitchen."

"You will?"

"Of course. Like you said, I'm drumming up business," he said cheerfully. He didn't know that I didn't have money to pay him to recreate my kitchen.

He put another shovelful of glass into the garbage bag. "What would you like to see in this space?" He waved a muscled tanned arm. "Come on, be creative."

"Anything?" I could play pretend.

"Anything."

"You know I like to cook, right?" I mentioned.

"Nope. Didn't know that. I like to cook too. Aerie not so much."

I walked to the middle of the room, crushing shards of glass under my sneakers. "I would put a farmer's sink right here." I motioned. I pushed a dark curl of my hair out of my face. "With a dishwasher, which wasn't here before. Gas stove in the corner—a commercial gas stove," I amended, "with an electric oven. Cabinets along the top." I waved my hand. "But not too high. The pantry over here. And a coffee and tea station over there."

"Sounds perfect. Let's make it happen."

"Really?" I put my arms down and turned toward him. "You'll really help me?"

He smiled. "What am I doing right now?"

"Thank you, Jay." I tried not to be too obvious about how much I enjoyed being around him.

"Not a problem. Let's get this cleaned up first. Then I can have one of my guys come by and pick up the damaged appliances. I'll see if I can get you any cash if we are able to resell them."

"Resell them?" I looked at the charred remains of an ancient refrigerator.

He eyed the oven which had definitely seen better days. "You never know. Antique dealers might want to pick something up." He smirked.

I looked at him in disbelief. "It's going to smell like smoked ham."

His eyes sparkled as he laughed. "Maybe that's what they're looking for."

I laughed along with him.

We cleaned up the kitchen until it resembled an organized mess. Jay's biceps flexed as he pulled the refrigerator away from the wall. He stopped. "I'll go downstairs and make sure the electricity and the water are turned off."

I totally missed what he was saying. "What?"

"I'm going into the basement to turn off the electricity before I unplug the appliances. The firemen should have done it already, but I want to make sure."

I nodded. "Safety first." I needed to be less obvious about ogling him in the future. I shook my head and swept the remaining debris from the melted linoleum floor. I wouldn't miss its greenish yellow design, that's for sure.

I pushed the broom behind the fridge and heard a metallic sound as I pulled the broom across the floor. I couldn't spot anything in the debris, but as I picked up the dustpan, I noticed a key. An old-style brass key with an ornately decorated handle. Long and slender, it was a lovely golden-brown color and cool to the touch. A nice antique of days gone by. I slipped it in my pocket as Jay came into the kitchen.

"Everything is turned off," he announced with a grin.

"Oh, good. We won't electrocute ourselves." Goodness knows I didn't need to add that to my list of dramas.

Jay quickly turned serious. "With everything that's gone on here, I think you better knock on wood."

We both knocked on the wall.

"There. All better." He resumed his easy attitude. Jay unplugged the fridge and I pushed at the oven until I could reach the plug. "What about this?" I pointed to the gas connection.

"I didn't bring any tools. I'll have one of my guys disconnect the gas when they take the appliances."

Jay and I taped some industrial plastic against the opening into the dining room to block it off from the rest of the house.

"Lucky it's spring, it'll only get warmer. You won't freeze. But I can bring some plywood the next time to make it secure. We should be able to frame everything up pretty quickly for you."

"Jay, thanks. Really. I don't know what I would have done." I didn't know how I could thank him enough. Not only did he help me with this mess and promise to help fix it, but he did it all while cheering me up too. I closed my eyes for a second and reminded myself I shouldn't fall for him. Not after what happened with the last guy. But I couldn't help it. I opened my eyes to see him subtly grinning at me.

"What?" I had to have soot on my nose or something.

He stopped grinning. "Nothing. Let's go back to the house and clean up. I think Robbie is making a Maryland crab soup today for the lunch rush."

We packed things up, but I noticed he wouldn't look me in the eye again. Great. I shook my head. I was reading into things. I needed to forget all about flirting and relationships and just move on with the work I had to do here to fix up this house.

8

After a bowl of Maryland crab soup that would make a Terp cry, Jay let me back into his house. I picked up my toiletries and Arnold. We headed back to the house that I kept moving into and out of over and over again.

I opened the front door and put Arnold on the floor.

And back again. He announced.

I put down the cardboard box he was using for litter and his dish of water. "Yes, I know. Hopefully, this will be the last time."

Snowball, that fur-ball of a cat, is likely to pitch a fit if I show up again. She's very private about her territory. She had all these rules for me to follow.

"Did you follow them?"

No. He licked his paw.

"Was that why she was spitting at you this morning?"

Arnold licked his other paw. *She was upset because I put my paw in her water dish.*

"You did it on purpose, didn't you?"

He turned and looked at me for a second and rubbed his

face on the one and only chair that stood in the room. *Of course, I did. Did you see how excited she got? It was hysterical.*

"Remind me to leave you over here next time."

Gladly. Clara told me I can have the run of the place, including the attic.

I stopped breathing for a second. "Who's Clara?" My voice shook because I knew the answer, and I really, really didn't want it to be true.

Clara, you know, the woman who helped me get you out of the house the other night.

I flashed back to the moment when I felt hands pushing me up out of bed and through the house until I got to the front door. I sat on the floor and stared at the ceiling. Wishing it not to be true. I laughed wryly.

"Who was I to think I could get away from it?" I told myself. Denial seemed to be my personal mantra. A fixer-upper? Easy. No money? Not a problem. I had seen the ghost; she had talked to me. But still, I wanted to pretend I was in a place where none of this nonsense existed. I shouted my frustration. "Ha, ha, very funny, Universe. Thank you very much. The joke's on me."

After all, the whole point of moving out was to get away from my crazy old life, not to find some new kind of crazy.

She says you're welcome. Arnold added nonchalantly.

"Who?"

Clara.

I pressed the palms of my hands to my eyes and laid back on the floor. "No, no, no. This is not supposed to happen." I rocked to and fro like a three-year-old in a temper tantrum. "I moved away from all of this for a reason."

Arnold ignored me and walked over to his dish and

lapped up some water. He laid down on the ancient braided rug, put his hind leg in the air and began to clean his nether regions.

So that's what he thinks of my own self-determination. I rolled my eyes at him, and decided, "If I choose not to believe it, it doesn't exist."

The window slammed shut.

I jerked around; my heart raced.

Arnold hadn't moved.

I forced myself to calm down. Breathe in, breathe out. I closed my eyes. I'll keep my beliefs to myself. I still refused to admit a ghost could live here too. I simply rejected the concept.

I should have expected it, but was still surprised when, at around midnight, the singing started. The fact that it was all in my head made me feel simultaneously insane and intruded upon.

By 3 a.m., as stubborn as I wanted to be, I desperately craved sleep, so after the twenty-third refrain of a song about listening to some mockingbird, I acquiesced.

"Fine. You live here too." And just like that, silence. Beautiful, golden silence and I drifted off to sleep. But I swore the next morning I'd refuse to admit to anyone, that a ghost lived with me even if she had a part in saving my life.

AFTER A THANKFULLY GHOST-FREE yoga lesson and shower, Aerie and I headed to the diner. I was sure if I could talk to a few more people today I could find out something about Becca's murder. Realizing this town has more secrets than a season of Game of Thrones, I knew someone had to know something. I just had to be persistent. Aerie slowed as we got closer to the diner.

"What's wrong?" I asked, thinking she had forgotten something back at the community center. I looked up and saw Mrs. Orsa standing outside the diner's front door, impatiently waiting.

"Robbie usually opens for me by six." Aerie's voice tightened. "He's never late." She ran up to the front door and looked in as she pulled out her keys.

"Where's Robbie?" Mrs. Orsa asked. Aerie unlocked the door and pulled it open. The inside of the diner was dark.

I waved a hand to invite Mrs. Orsa. "Come on in, you can have a seat while we get things started."

Aerie flipped on the lights. "Robbie?" She walked to the back of the kitchen. "He's not here." She waved me over. She took out her cell phone from the hip pocket of her yoga pants. "I'm calling him."

The diner was eerily quiet without the sound of cooking food and dishes clashing with silverware.

"Robbie, are you okay?"

Her voice became tentative. "Okay, we'll see you in a few minutes. If you need to take the day off, I'll understand."

"Okay. Yes. I'll start the grill. But Robbie I'm serious, if you need a personal day, I can manage the diner."

"Okay, see you soon."

Gas wooshed into the grill as she turned it on. She came out of the kitchen looking confused. "He said he just 'ran into an issue this morning' but he'd be coming in."

"Is he okay?"

"He swears he is, but he didn't sound okay."

I helped Aerie set the tables, wipe down the counter, and plug in the milk shake maker and the juke box.

When Robbie came in, we both stared at him. "What happened to your eye?"

He reacted like he didn't even know he had the world's biggest shiner on his right eye. He reached up and almost touched his face but thought better of it and put his hand back down. "This? Oh, I uh, hit my head on a cabinet door in my kitchen. Stupid really." He put on his apron. "I'm really sorry I'm late. It won't happen again."

Robbie disappeared into the kitchen and started frying up the bacon and sausage patties.

I looked at Aerie. She didn't believe him either, but customers started coming in for the breakfast rush and I quickly made my way to follow him into the kitchen.

"I hope the other guy looks worse."

He focused on flipping the bacon, but a hint of a grin on his face disappeared as soon as I saw it.

I grabbed a muffin, wondered if it was vegan, and scarfed it down before heading back out to help Aerie with the orders.

The breakfast rush was fast paced but short lived. The crabby lady, Mrs. Orsa, sat alone, fumbling through a plate of scrambled eggs. At the moment she looked serene; her face wasn't pinched up with frustration at the world, and I wondered what kind of person she was behind her grumpy facade. I wanted to find out. She was drinking tea and not coffee so I grabbed the pot of hot water and headed her way.

"Can I freshen that up for you?" I held up the pot of water. "And another tea bag?"

"I could use more hot water, but don't waste the tea. I can reuse this one."

I poured water to fill her mug.

"Thank you."

"You're welcome, Mrs. Orsa. Have a good morning."

"Small chance of that today," she groused.

I had to ask. "Oh? Why is that?"

"My son is asking for things he shouldn't and causing me more grief than a mother should have to manage."

"Well, if there's anything I can do to help, Mrs. Orsa, just let me know."

"No need, no need." She brushed her lips with her napkin, folded it, and placed it on the table.

"Would you like your check now?"

"Please." She made her way out of the booth and stood. I handed her a slip with the amount. She gave me a ten. "Keep the change." She winked at me.

"Good luck, Mrs. Orsa."

She grinned. "I'm glad you're the one who bought the house. I know you'll take good care of it."

"Oh, okay." I watched as she left the diner.

Robbie started the lunch's soup option. I finished loading dishes into the dishwasher after breakfast. He seemed to be rushing, chopping the vegetables, and tossing them haphazardly into the huge pot on the stove.

"Mira, this needs to cook for one to two hours on low." He showed me the setting on the stove.

"Okay." Not sure what he was getting at.

"I have a few errands to run before lunch, but they're in the city. If I'm not back in time this will be ready to go by then."

"Oh, okay Robbie, no problem."

"Thanks." He didn't look up. Just took off his apron, hung it, and left through the back door which emptied into the back parking lot. I watched him go, realizing that he hadn't said anything to Aerie.

Odd.

The dishwasher beeped; it had completed its cycle. I opened it up and steam poured out toward the ceiling. I pondered why Robbie was being so secretive about the black eye, and why he wouldn't tell Aerie that he might not be back for lunch.

I gingerly took out the hot dishes and stacked them on the shelves in their correct locations. Robbie kept a very ordered kitchen.

Aerie came in with another bucket of dirty dishes. I unloaded, brushed the food into the compost bin in the corner near the door, and setup the dishwasher for another load. I might as well tell her. "Robbie said he had errands to run."

She turned toward me. "Really? Okay. I guess." She glanced at the back door.

"He started the soup, but he gave me instructions in case he was late."

"Late? What is going on? First a black eye and now he might not be back for the lunch hour?" She sounded hurt and upset.

Robbie seemed friendly but I was new here I didn't know him any better than the next person that walked in the door of the diner. "This is out of character for him?"

"It's so not like Robbie. I would never believe he would get into a fight with anyone, ever. He is so mild mannered. It just doesn't make sense."

"How long have you known him?" I closed the hood to the dishwasher and started the cycle.

"He's been here a while. My mom hired him. Why didn't he tell me he needed some time off? I would have understood." Aerie's voice rang with injured feelings.

"Does he have any family around?"

"No. The only other person I've seen him talk with is Ellie; she's his neighbor."

That seemed like the next logical place for me to visit. I wondered if Ellie knew any more about Robbie than Aerie did.

"Okay, so I'm panicking a little bit." Aerie fidgeted with her piece of chalk.

"Um, do you really not know how to cook, Aerie?"

Even though both Aerie and Jay had hinted about this, she did own the town's diner. It was really hard to believe she couldn't cook at all. "Not even a little bit?"

"Jay always cooks when Robbie is sick."

I giggled. "I can cook. Not as good as Robbie, but I can manage. And he did leave the soup. He'll probably be back anyway."

Aerie took in a deep breath. "Okay, good because otherwise we'd be in big trouble. I'd burn everything for sure."

"You wouldn't be that bad."

"Oh, really? You should talk to Jay about that. He'll set the record straight. Trust me, I can't cook." She put her hands up in defense.

"We'll do okay today. I promise." I checked the flame level under the soup pot. Low boil, and it smelled like broccoli cheese. My stomach growled.

"Mira? Thanks for helping me out. I know you don't have to." Her worried look made me feel for her.

"You've been a great friend since I got here, and Jay's been helping me with the repairs at my house. So, it's all good. No worries." The least I could do was help her get through the rest of today if Robbie didn't show up.

"I'll go back out and take orders." She peered into the dining room. "Thankfully, it's slowing down."

"Good, then we don't have to worry." Although I could cook my grandma's pierogi and cabbage rolls, the last time I worked in a restaurant was when I was sixteen, and I wasn't allowed in the kitchen. I didn't have the abject terror that Aerie had about cooking, so that was something.

As it happened, Ellie stopped by for an egg sandwich, something I could easily whip up, and the police chief came in for a cup of coffee. Aerie handled the drinks, so when he placed his order I rushed out from the kitchen.

"Officer Orsa, have you been able to find out anything about the fire?"

"It's *Chief* Orsa. And you'll hear about it when the rest of the world hears about it." He paid the exact amount for his cup of coffee, minus a tip and left the diner without even looking at me.

"He's usually blunt, but that was an all-time high." Aerie put the money in the cash drawer. "Speaking of Jay..." Her smile had a devious look to it.

"We were speaking of Jay?" I blushed. I already knew what she was going to say. I backed up into the kitchen and hit my hip on the counter. I wanted to hide.

"What do you think of my brother?" she coyly inquired.

"I think Jay is awesome for helping me with the house."

"And..." She insinuated more with her tone.

"You're fishing for something." I stopped and fumbled with the sugar shaker on the counter.

"Do you like him?" Her grin was huge. "...because he likes you."

"What?" I knocked over the sugar shaker and it spilled across the counter.

Aerie leaned forward and righted it while I stared. "He said he had fun over at your place. And as much as Jay loves construction tasks, cleaning up is not one of them."

Aerie brushed up the sugar.

"You think he likes me?" I was a bit surprised.

Her eyes lit up, giddy. "You do like him!'

I nodded guiltily.

"I'm totally going to set you guys up on a date." She brushed the sugar into the compost bin.

"No, no, don't do that."

"Why not?"

"My history with men is not a good one. I swore when I moved out here, I would take a break from relationships."

She waved off my objections. "This is my brother, he's a great guy. You'll see."

"I already see," I said under my breath. Jay was not only good looking but kind and generous and funny. And probably the downfall of my independence. "I just can't. Not right now."

"You're sure?" Her giddiness subsided slightly.

I nodded.

I didn't want to, but it was for my own good, and his as well. I needed to find my own space in the world right now. And my plan was to fix up this house and sell it and move on. No attachments. No relationships. I looked over at Aerie with remorse. I would miss her when I left. But at this rate it would take a long time to get the house in shape to sell.

"You don't have to commit to anything now. Keep an open mind, okay?" She nudged my arm.

"Maybe." Because secretly the idea of dating Jay made my knees weak. I wanted to throw caution to the wind, so I changed the subject before I could change my mind. "I was thinking of heading over to the bank to talk to Ellie. If she lives near Robbie, maybe she saw something."

"That's a good idea. Let's find out if she's heard

something from anyone else in town...you know, the rumor mill."

"You'll be okay alone?"

"As long as no one wants me to use the grill we're all good until the lunch rush starts."

"I'll be back as soon as I can." I hung up my apron and any idea of dating Jay, and headed out the door.

9

A light drizzle had started, and by the time I got to the bank, it was a downpour; my hair was dripping, and my clothes were damp.

I stepped into the foyer and immediately regretted it. The temperature in the room would cause icicles to form on my nose if the a/c blasted any higher. My wet clothes felt like they had been placed in a refrigerator.

Ellie jumped up when she saw me and dropped the book she was reading. "Hold on, I'll get you something." She disappeared into the back and returned with a gym towel.

"Thanks." I wiped my wet arms and ran the towel through my hair. "I thought it would only sprinkle a bit."

"They sell umbrellas over at the General Store, along with like, everything else."

"Good to know. Thanks." I offered the towel back and she hung it over one of the waiting chairs in the foyer.

"What can I help you with today, Mira?"

"With all the stuff about my house..."

"You mean like how it's haunted?"

"It's not haunted." I refused to admit this. To anyone except my cat and the ghost herself, at least.

"Someone died there and then it caught on fire." She looked at me as if it was obvious that these two things would lead a place to be haunted.

"It isn't haunted. But I am interested to know more about the history of the property."

"You mean who owned it in the past?"

"Yes. Or anything else that you've heard."

Ellie glanced toward the back room where I assume her manager was sitting. She whispered, "I can look for something in the files over my lunch break, just not right now."

"I understand. Thanks, I appreciate it."

"But I can tell you, that house has been empty for more than twenty years. Last I heard I thought the town had bought it. Poor Becca probably could've told you more."

I nodded solemnly. I let the topic drop. I didn't expect to get any more information until she was able to look at some paperwork. Unless...

"Do you know Robbie, the chef over at the diner?"

"Yeah, but not really. He's kind of a loner. Doesn't have any family in town." She walked back around the counter and sat down.

"Aerie mentioned that he's your neighbor?"

"Yeah, I usually see him when he mows his lawn, but he usually has earbuds in, so he doesn't chat."

Dead end. "Well, thanks anyway."

"What's going on. Isn't he at the diner?"

"He left under odd circumstances today, so I just wanted to ask around."

"Do you want me to keep an eye on his house for you... kind of like a spy?" I could hear excitement in her voice.

"No, Ellie, I don't think that's a good idea." But I could tell she saw the gleam in my eye, that said, *just don't get caught.*

I grinned at her conspiratorially. "Any other interesting news lately?"

Ellie glanced left and right as if someone was listening in, even though we were the only ones here. She leaned forward. "If I were you, I would stay away from that Jay character."

I took a step back. "Why?"

"He was the last person I saw with Becca. Some kind of date or something—" she raised her eyebrows— "if you know what I mean."

I couldn't breathe. I squeaked out, "Oh?" My impression of Jay suddenly toppled.

Ellie continued, "Which is interesting because I thought she was dating someone else. I saw Becca and Jay drive out of town together the day of the murder." She grinned like she'd been holding on to that information like gold.

Mr. Meyer, the bank manager, stormed out from his back-room office. "Ms. Bracken, what have I told you about talking about the customers?" He waggled his finger. "This is a place of business, not the town rumor mill."

I needed fresh air. Immediately. "I gotta go." I hustled my way out of the bank. Jay was the last to see Becca? He had appeared, eerily enough, right there outside my house when the kitchen exploded. My knees buckled and I caught myself. I needed to sit down.

Things began to fall into place on the walk home. I couldn't face Aerie at the diner just yet. I had some time before the lunch rush. Home would make me feel better but once I walked inside, I noticed the plastic tarp that Jay had taped up over the gaping hole where the kitchen used to be.

The night of the explosion, he had been at my house. As soon as I was out of the house, he had been right there waiting for me. Or was he waiting to make sure the explosion that he set went off? Why else would he have been at my house in the middle of the night?

And what about Becca? Ellie said they were dating. Had she broken it off with him and he got violent? I shuddered. The possibility that the kind person I had gotten to know over the last few days could have a dark side, shocked me. Dark enough to murder someone. I felt sick. I needed water. I found a bottle of water and made it to the powder room. I drank a mouthful and sat on the lid of the toilet gulping more water.

Arnold worked the door open and rubbed against my leg. He looked up and meowed. "I know buddy, it's one heck of a mess."

He rubbed against my other leg to comfort me.

"A mess only I could get into, huh?"

He jumped into my lap and sat up looking me straight in the eye. *You're always getting into a mess. Let's call Darla.*

I took a deep breath and let my shoulders drop back to where they were supposed to be. The stress of this week was going to pin them permanently to my ears. I breathed in, breathed out.

You should confront him about damaging your territory.

"Who? Jay?" I didn't know if I could do that.

You need to rough him up, let him know this is your territory not his.

"Arnold, I am not a cat, and neither is Jay."

Aerie shares his territory with that Snowball, right?

"I should talk to Aerie." The thought made me nauseous and I filled the glass again and sipped. "I don't know if I can."

You must defend your territory. Or I have taught you nothing.

Arnold was obviously having a moment of grandeur. "What exactly are you talking about? You've never taught me anything."

Then I should. Immediately. Go to their territory, er...house, and slash him with your claws. It's sends the right message.

"You've gone crazy. I'm not slashing anyone." But I did have to talk to Aerie. I sighed. "I'm not good with confrontation."

If you don't do any confronting, you might be the next murder victim in this town.

He had a very good point.

I don't want anything bad to happen to you. He purred and nuzzled me.

"Aw, thanks." I reached out to pet him in my lap. "Let's get you some treats."

Because then he'll take over your territory and I won't have anywhere to go.

"Thanks a lot." I still gave him a treat because he's my cat, and secretly I know he loves me. I located his box of cat food, toys, and treats and pulled out a zip-locked bag. When fed him a few, he inhaled them.

"Don't you want to chew and enjoy them?"

He meowed and slowly licked his kitty lips.

How could I tell Aerie that I thought her brother might be a killer? The same man who had been so kind to help me fix the kitchen. The kitchen he may have destroyed, I reminded myself. Then my brain flashed a picture of Becca laying on my kitchen floor dead. My entire body shivered.

If I didn't say anything, I might very well end up being the next victim.

I checked my watch. It was 11:45 a.m. The start of the

lunch hour. I took a deep breath. As much as I didn't think I could do it, I'd have to go back to the diner. I couldn't leave Aerie to handle the lunch crowd by herself. Not if Robbie wasn't back.

Could Jay have done something to Robbie?

Robbie had shown up with a black eye and if he hasn't come back...

Enough. It was time to head over to the diner. I'd help Aerie with the lunch rush and then when we closed up, I would tell her what I'd found out. I only hoped I didn't run into Jay before then.

10

L uckily the lunch shift kept us hopping. There was no sign of Robbie, but his soup was delicious. I managed to keep filling all the orders and by the end of the lunch shift, I would have felt really satisfied with a job well done, if I hadn't been wondering the whole time how I was going to tell my new best friend that her brother was a murderer and arsonist. Even though we were run ragged, my stilted one-word answers to Aerie's questions had her wondering what was going on.

She came up to me with her hands on her hips. "What's up?"

"We have to talk, privately."

She leaned closer. "What did you find out?"

"Nothing good. Can we go to your house?" Did I really want to be in Jay's house for this?

If everything imploded, I wanted to be able to leave and head home.

Aerie packed up a few sandwiches and the last of the vegan donuts. She handed me the keys and I locked up. It was 2:45 p.m.

"What time is Jay getting back?"

Her eyes lit up. "You've changed your mind. You want me to set you up?" She danced around me until she saw my face.

"No, Aerie, look, let's get to the house and talk. How long do you think it will be before he gets home?"

"He said he'd be home early and that usually means about four or five p.m."

"Okay, we'll have time to talk."

Aerie looked uncomfortable. But not as uncomfortable as she was about to be when I shared my suspicions.

We walked to her house and sat in the kitchen.

Aerie looked me over. "Your aura is all kinds of swirling. Are you feeling okay?"

It would be best if I started from the beginning. "You know I've been trying to find information about the house, and about Becca to see if anything links to the explosion."

Aerie nodded.

"I talked to Detective Lockheart...well, I tried to talk to him. As a detective I'm sure he's good, but he certainly doesn't like to share information."

"That's just Dan. He's been like that since he was a kid. Nice guy, just doesn't share."

I kept forgetting that everyone here knew each other and knew each other since, like, kindergarten. I nodded. "He was mad that Jay was touching everything at the crime scene." I paid close attention to her to see if she had any kind of reaction.

"He works in construction; he was probably making sure everything was safe before people entered the kitchen."

It was obvious that Aerie didn't know about Becca and Jay. "The detective made some comment about Jay being my boyfriend. Was Jay in a relationship recently?"

87

"No, he hasn't mentioned anyone—that's why I want to hook you guys up."

My stomach turned and my face burned. I just couldn't keep this up. "Look, Aerie, I talked to Ellie, she said Jay and Becca were dating."

She looked surprised.

"She saw them together the day of the murder."

"But Jay... He would tell me if he was seeing someone." She turned away and stood pushing the chair away from the table.

"You don't sound so sure."

"Well, he's been kind of standoffish lately, which isn't like him." She paced the floor.

"Jay was the last one to see Becca, I think, that day. And he was messing with the crime scene after the fire."

Aerie's eyes widened at my words and I could tell she came to the same conclusion that I had. Aerie rubbed her hands over her face. "Jay can't kill anyone. He just can't."

"What if it was an accident? Detective Lockheart says they're still waiting on the autopsy to find out the cause of death."

Aerie stood, pushing the chair away and began to pace back and forth. She rubbed her arms as if she was cold. "He hasn't been talking to me lately... He's been different. Distant."

I thought telling Aerie, getting it out, would somehow help me in some way. But I felt horrible. Aerie was second guessing someone she loved, and watching her go through this made me miserable.

"When the explosion happened, Jay was right there. Outside my house."

She nodded. "I sent him to check on you because something just felt wrong." She shook her head. "But what if he went into the kitchen..." Aerie leaned on the table, staring into empty space, then sat hard on the floor. "Oh. He was the one to check the kitchen windows the night we left you."

I went to the sink and poured her a glass of water. She sipped it slowly and handed me the glass when she finished.

"Where's my cell phone?"

It sat on the table where she had left it and I handed it to her.

Her hands shook as she scrolled and pressed the screen. Her voice trembled. "Jay, I need you to come home right away... Yes. Yes. Something is very wrong. Come home." She pushed the red End Call and handed me her phone. She stood and pulled out her hair tie, smoothed the hair out of her face and pulled it back up into a tight knot. She took a deep breath. "We're going to find out the truth."

Neither of us could talk. We sat in silence and waited.

Jay showed up twenty minutes later looking frantic. Once he spotted Aerie sitting calmly across from me at the kitchen table, his face darkened. "What's going on? You sounded like someone died."

"Someone has; Becca," Aerie said in a tone I had never heard her use before. She pushed back her chair and stood across from Jay. She was a few inches shorter than her brother, but her fury certainly made up for it.

"Ellie told Mira you were dating Becca."

"What?" Jay shot me a confused glance. "What are you talking about?"

"She said she saw you with Becca the day of the murder." Aerie crossed her arms and stood waiting.

"I wasn't dating Becca."

"Then what were you doing with her the day of the murder?" Her face reddened.

Jay rubbed his hand across his forehead. "I didn't want you to find out this way."

"Find out?" Aerie's hands turned into fists and she shouted. "Jay, what happened?"

"I *was* with Becca the day of her murder." He stuck his hands in his pockets but continued to look at the floor. "I told Dan. The police know."

Aerie brought her right foot down on the linoleum floor with a thump. "Jay, you tell me right now what happened!"

Jay shook his head. "Becca drove me out to look at some property."

Aerie stared at her brother. "You what?"

"I want to move out Air. I want my own place. Becca was going to help me find some land that I could build a house on."

Aerie's fists at her side relaxed. "Why? Why do you want to move out?"

"For starters, this house has too many memories for me. Since Mom and Dad... were out of the picture it's felt different. I don't know what to say. I just...I need a new place."

"Why didn't you tell me?"

"Because one of the reasons I want to get my own place is because I am dating Chelsea."

Aerie's eyes flared with renewed anger. "You're dating *her*? After everything that happened?"

"You see, this is why I didn't tell you." Jay turned and paced to the other end of the kitchen.

"Why would you date her?" Aerie pleaded.

"She's changed, Aerie. And I've changed." Jay grabbed his keys. "I can't believe you would think that I had anything to do with Becca's murder." Jay shook his head. "I'm going over to Dan's." Jay yanked the door open so hard that it hit the wall and broke the plaster. He revved the engine then pulled his truck away from the front of the house. Tires squealed as he drove away.

I could barely breathe. I was so wrong. "Aerie, I'm sorry. I'm so, so sorry."

Aerie's lips pinched into a tight white line. She shook her head and walked upstairs.

As I sat alone in the kitchen, I wondered how I could have been so wrong. Jay wasn't a murderer. I needed to learn to trust my instincts. Jay was a good guy. Now I was more determined than ever to find out who murdered Becca. Not only so I could clear my conscience but so that Jay would forgive me.

11

When I got home, Arnold was right there to greet me with a leg rub. I bent down and scratched under his chin. "Hey, buddy."

You don't appear injured. You've won the confrontation?

I closed and locked the door and sat on the floor in front of Arnold. "I messed up." He purred and rubbed my head with his. "I should have known better." I took a deep breath and sighed.

Arnold curled up in my lap and I stroked his furry head. He looked up at me with big golden eyes. *Did you lose our territory?*

"No. Worse. I shouldn't have said anything to Aerie or Jay. Now they both hate me. What kind of person accuses the people who are helping them of murder?" I stood and picked up Arnold and snuggled him against my shoulder as I walked into the dining room. "Now we still don't know who it is."

Arnold squirmed and meowed. *Then we must continue to search.* I let him jump down.

I didn't have an appetite for dinner. Not that I had much

in the way of food or a kitchen in which to cook. I glanced over at the plastic that led to the burned-out kitchen. Jay had said he would get some plywood to cover this and make it safer for me.

I sighed again. I couldn't do much about anything right now. But I might as well be productive. I had laundry to wash and no one was going to do it for me.

"Come on, Arnold, let's get the clothes and see how that old washer works." If it works.

I climbed the tall steep steps to the bedroom and gathered up the loose clothes that I had thrown on the floor. At least my room would look cleaner now.

I shouldered my load and walked downstairs and through the hall, made a hard left, and opened the door to the basement. The musty smell reminded me of antiques and old hardware stores. I searched for a light switch, then remembered there wasn't one. I had to go down three or four stairs and reach up to pull the light bulb string. It clicked on, no problem, but I dropped a pair of pants and a shirt. I continued down the creaky stairs. I'd come back and pick them up.

The washer sat flush against the far wall, which was made of mortar and stone, not concrete, reminding me how much history this house had. I stuffed the clothes in the drum of the washer and realized I didn't have any detergent. Yep, not something I thought about bringing with me. "Well, I guess clean water can do something for these clothes."

Arnold rubbed his face against the side of the washer.

It smells like mice down here. I could have sworn he grinned as he rubbed his face on a beat-up cardboard box.

I went back up the stairs to retrieve the pants and shirt and shoved them into the washer, an old-style avocado green. Obviously made before I was born. If it was still functional, I'd give kudos to the manufacturer. I turned the knobs and pushed the button. Nothing happened.

No kudos, I guess.

And then it hit me. "Jay turned off the water so he could move the appliances in the kitchen the other day," I told Arnold. "Now to find the on-off valve. Hmmm."

I followed the skinny copper water pipe along the wall to the back corner. I had to climb over some wooden crates. Lots of leftover history in this house that I would have to investigate. But not right now.

Right now, I needed clean clothes. I climbed on the crates and leaned against the wall. One of the crates shifted. I grabbed onto the pipe to balance myself and was thankful for sturdy metal piping. I grabbed the overhead lever.

I pushed down on it. The lever didn't even squeak. I pushed up; it wouldn't budge.

"What the heck." Jay had managed to turn it off. I had a flash of his beautiful biceps but shook it out of my head, the man must hate me at this point.

I tried again, but nothing doing. I searched the basement looking for anything that could give me leverage. Or a hammer. I would pound it into submission. I was getting this laundry done tonight come hell or high water. I snickered at my own pun. I frowned, I didn't need any variety of high water in the basement, pun or otherwise.

I climbed down. A quick glance around the basement made me realize just how large it was, filled with antiques and objects left behind from previous owners.

Toward the front of the house, against the wall stood a workbench made entirely of wood, no nails, darkened with age, and a tack board that held a number of random tools.

Most were worn and some rusty. I saw the claw hammer right away and decided that was my best option.

I climbed back up on my perch next to the water valve and pounded on the lever. It moved ever so slightly. I banged on it some more, venting all the day's frustration, until it lined up with the pipe.

I climbed down from the wooden crates, the hammer clutched firmly in my hand. The hammer should go back to its resting spot before I caused any damage. With the way my day was going I couldn't be sure. I put it back in place, hanging it on the wall behind the workbench, and returned to the washer. This time when I pulled the start knob out, the water poured into the drum. I closed the lid and gave it a gentle rub. "Good job, washer."

"Come on, Arnold, I'll see if I have any kitty treats for you upstairs." Or any treats for myself. The dinner hour had come and gone.

I wasn't halfway up the stairs before a rhythmic clunking began. A metallic banging that made me cringe. "I guess my luck hasn't changed."

I marched down the rest of the stairs, but the closer I got it sounded like something was loose inside the drum. I turned off the washer and opened the lid. I pulled out each piece of soaking wet clothing and hung it around the rim of the washer. The clink of something metal falling back into the drum caught my attention.

I rolled up my sleeve and reached into the cold water almost up to my shoulder and pulled out a key.

The key that I found in the kitchen when Jay and I had been cleaning up. I wondered if somewhere in the house this key had a lock.

The clothes were dripping a puddle on the floor and my arm was now chilled. I put the key on the shelf above the washer and stuffed all the clothes back into the drum. I closed the lid and started it again. No clanking noises.

I grinned, satisfied that I might have moderately clean clothes at the end of the hour. I shook my arm to dry it off. Arnold followed me avoiding the water droplets as I marched upstairs to look for a dry towel.

THE NEXT MORNING, I woke up with a start. A pounding sound reverberated from downstairs. I threw a sweatshirt over my pajama ensemble of t-shirt and sweatpants and cautiously made my way down the stairs. If someone was trying to break in, they were doing a pretty loud job of it.

It would be easy through the kitchen and that's where the sound came from. I searched the dining room for something to use as a weapon. The only thing I could find was a yoga mat that Aerie had let me bring home.

I walked carefully toward the hanging plastic that separated me from the intruder. I raised my arm with the yoga mat and silently pulled it back and charged.

And ran square into a broad chest.

"Oof."

It was Jay. I dropped the arm holding the mat.

He stepped back and looked at me quizzically, "You were going to brain me with a yoga mat?"

"I'm sorry." I fumbled around and put down the vinyl mat. "What are you doing here?"

"I promised I would help you fix this up, and I don't go back on my promises." He was starting to put up the plywood between the burned-out kitchen and my dining room. If I had walked through the plastic opening ten minutes later, I would have smacked into plywood.

"Jay about yesterday...I'm so sorry."

"Look, I said I would fix the kitchen." He turned his back to me and continued working. "But I am not in the mood to talk."

He could ignore me all he wanted but I was going to apologize because I meant it. "Jay, I shouldn't have jumped to conclusions. It was wrong of me to think that you had anything to do with Becca's death." I took another deep breath. "I just hope you'll forgive me."

Those last few words quivered in my throat. I didn't want him to see me upset so I turned on my heel and marched back into the house.

I took a quick icy cold shower and got dressed. No, I wasn't going to tell Jay I had a problem with the water heater.

I had one more person that I needed to apologize to. I glanced at my watch. She was probably back from her yoga class and headed to the Soup and Scoop. She would need me if Robbie was still missing.

"Okay, Arnold, you hold down the fort, I have a mea culpa to extend." I patted him on the head and then scratched his chin. "Wish me luck."

He meowed.

As I made my way toward the Soup and Scoop, I could see it was as busy as always. The bell over the door sounded as I pushed inside and found chaos. Aerie's head popped up from the kitchen. She looked frantic and worn-out. She was trying to flip over-easy eggs and I watched as the yolks split and ran down her spatula.

Without thinking I grabbed an apron from the hook and made my way into the kitchen. "What's going on?"

"Robbie didn't show up this morning. When I got here after yoga a line waited for me outside the door."

"He didn't call?"

"No." Her head perked up again as the bell rang. "Can you take orders?"

"Sure." I grabbed the mini chalkboard and chalk but then she tried to plate the eggs. I held out my open hand. "If you want, I can cook." The wave of relief that crossed her face made me feel better instantly.

She handed me the egg coated spatula and took the mini chalkboard and chalk. "Are you sure?"

I nodded. Even though I cooked for the lunch rush yesterday, I hadn't learned a ton about being a short-order chef. Everything had been prepped and labeled by Robbie, this was going to have to be all me, but I was determined to make it work for Aerie's sake. I glanced up at the large chalkboard where she usually put the orders for Robbie, but it was empty. I caught Aerie before she left the kitchen. "What are the orders?"

"Oh, right, sorry. They're all here." She tapped her temple. She quickly reached up and scribbled out six orders.

Okay, mostly eggs and bacon. I could handle those. After half a dozen broken attempts I understood the appeal of the vegan egg mixture that didn't have yolks that broke in a slurry mess. I had to hunt for the saltshaker, and I found that behind a pitcher of batter. A quick sniff told me it was for pancakes. Thank goodness I wouldn't have to mix it myself.

The first batch of pancakes was a disaster. Batter oozed everywhere on the grill. I realized I needed to turn up the heat. Only on one section. Because when I turned the heat up on the whole grill, it burned the next batch of eggs. After a bit more practice, the nightmare abated, and I almost felt like a pro until I dropped a large bottle of imitation maple syrup on my foot.

Aerie heard me curse and ran into the kitchen. "Are you okay?" She picked up a bottle from the floor and placed it on the opposite counter. She pulled the elastic tie out of my hair and smoothed back my curls, like a proper mother hen. Then she tied my hair back up, and gave me a big hug. "Thank you so much, Mira. You have no idea how much I appreciate this."

I took a deep breath. "I want to apologize for yesterday, I shouldn't have accused Jay. He would never do anything like that."

"He wouldn't. But he has been acting very strangely over the last few weeks." She helped me flip some bacon that started to scorch. "I still can't believe he's dating Chelsea." She shook her head.

"Sounds like there's a story there?" I inquired.

"Yes." She glanced at the customers out front. "But not now. Let's wait until after the breakfast rush. Most people are finishing up."

No more orders came in, so I went out front and helped Aerie bus tables.

We didn't talk until the last customer left. "The story about Chelsea goes back to when we were kids." Aerie took a deep breath and let it out. "I try to pretend I'm over it. And I work really hard at it too. You know, with the meditation and yoga." She paused and wiped down a table. "But when we were kids, Chelsea was a bully. And she bullied me—only me—constantly."

She scrubbed harder on the next table. "Just when I think I'm over the whole situation, every time I hear her name, I feel like I'm twelve again." She picked up the plastic bin of dishes and hustled it into the kitchen.

The slam of it against the stainless-steel counter reverberated through the empty diner.

She came back out with her hands on her hips. "I just don't understand why Jay would *date* her."

Until that moment I hadn't realized how upset I had been to find out that he was seeing someone. Of course, I had vowed to avoid relationships. And yet I felt drawn to Jay, and I must have hoped that he had felt something for me too. Obviously not. Clearly, I had to keep reminding myself, I was not looking for a man.

"He did say that she had changed. When was the last time you talked to her?"

Aerie paced the floor and tugged at her apron. "Never."

In the short time I had known her I had never seen Aerie this agitated.

"Chelsea worked with Becca. She's one of the realtors at that company."

"Well, then maybe she knows the last person that Becca had talked to the day of the murder."

"Or maybe I can talk her out of dating my brother." A mischievous glint sparkled in her eye as her hand tightened into a fist.

I had the sinking suspicion that gentle Aerie had another side.

"Let's go talk to her. I need to find out what happened with Becca so that I can figure out who set fire to my house."

"We have about an hour before the soup needs to be ready for lunch." Aerie untied her apron and hung it up. "Let's go."

I just hoped I wouldn't have to referee any kind of cat fight.

12

Aerie gave directions while I drove, although I had a vague memory of the first time I was out here and made the decision to buy the house. It felt like ages ago. The Buick played nice today and took us where we wanted to go. The realtor building stood on the other side of town in a small one-story building. A bell rang as we entered the office.

Two desks filled the impeccably homey space and one sat empty. That desk must have been Becca's, my poor realtor. The woman at the other desk stood expectantly.

Her strawberry blonde hair was expertly coiffed at her shoulders and her makeup was flawless. Her forced smile was about as fake as they come. "Good morning ladies, can I help you?"

From the tone of her voice she was actually saying, *What the heck are you doing here,* and, *how soon before you leave.* In reality, she continued to smile.

Surprisingly, Aerie stepped forward. "Hi, Chelsea. We are wondering if you can answer a few questions for us."

Chelsea waved a less-than-welcoming hand to the two

chairs that sat in front of her desk. "Great. What can I help you with?"

"First, I want to know why you are dating my brother." Aerie's tone was menacing.

I placed a hand on her arm. "Actually, we were wondering if you could give us some insight into Becca's schedule the day of the murder."

"Look, I can date who ever I want. And as for Becca, I told the police everything I knew." She stood. "So, unless you two are planning to buy a house I suggest you get out of here, now."

I stood up. "Someone broke into my house and set fire to the kitchen. Probably to cover up whatever evidence was left behind from the murder. It's kind of personal."

Aerie's mouth dropped open as she realized something. "You got a promotion, didn't you, now that Becca is dead?"

Chelsea sat back down, obviously realizing it was in her best interest to share what she knew. "That morning Becca met with Jay." She glared at Aerie.

Aerie continued her interrogation. "Why weren't you the one showing Jay the property that day? Why would he give the commission to Becca and not his girlfriend?" I could tell that last word caused her throat to tighten.

"I think he was planning to surprise me. But obviously that went out the window when Becca was killed."

Aerie flushed red and her lips tightened.

The right side of Chelsea's mouth turned up. "As I was saying, her first appointment was with Jay. Later she was supposed to meet *you* at your house. But obviously that didn't happen." She made it sound like she was accusing me of something. I immediately understood Chelsea had a skill set that screamed *Bully*. Jay claimed she had changed—

maybe toward him, but it was clear the animosity between Aerie and Chelsea still existed.

"She made it to the house," I added.

"Well, her car wasn't there, was it?" Chelsea leaned back in her chair.

"What?" Aerie and I responded at the same time.

"Like I said, I told the police everything I knew. But her car was still here. So, she must have met someone here and left with them." She stood. "Now, if you ladies are done. I can do some real work."

Aerie and I stood. I noticed a little bit of fire still in Aerie's eye. I took hold of her hand and she let out a breath. "You had better be good to my brother. Or I'll..."

"Our relationship is between him and me, not him and his sister." Chelsea used a snarky tone.

Just then the door opened. We all turned as Jay stepped into the office. At first, he appeared confused, then angry. "What are you two doing here?"

Before I could say anything, Aerie jumped in, "We were just having a chat."

Jay marched across the room. "Right. How about the two of you stay out of my personal life?"

"We were asking some questions about Becca. I'm trying to figure out—"

"And leave Chelsea alone. She has nothing to do with this. Jay walked around the desk and took Chelsea by the arm. "Come on, honey, let's go."

Aerie flinched. But then, so did I. It was one thing to hear my new crush was dating someone; it was another to hear him call that someone "honey" in front of me. I had to remind myself that Jay had never been mine. Why was I having these stupid feelings?

Chelsea waved a manicured finger toward us. "These two have to leave first so I can lock up."

Jay gave both of us a death glare and we quickly made our way out of the office.

Once in the car, Aerie's first words were, "I am so sorry for that." She shifted in her seat. "That woman brings out the worst in me."

"Well, she brings out the worst in me too and I only just met her." I put on my seatbelt and started the engine. "Now what?"

"We go back to the diner. Do you know how to make soup?"

"Robbie didn't leave anything, like in the fridge?"

"I hope you're creative."

"Let's shoot for edible."

WE ARRIVED BACK at the diner at eleven-thirty. Nowhere near enough time to get ready for the lunch crush.

"We'll need to hurry. Do you know what to do about the soup?"

I stared at Aerie; my mouth twitched. "I can make something I'm sure, but when it comes to restaurant cooking, the closest comparison I have is watching those cooking shows on TV."

My words eased the nervous look on her face but made my belly ache from shear fear. I repeated a version of the mantra I adopted when I left Massachusetts. Whatever it takes, I can do this myself. After all, I knew how to cook. I could do this.

We hustled out of the car and went inside. Thankfully, there was no one waiting in line.

Aerie laid out the silverware and napkins on the tables while I went back to check the kitchen refrigerator in more detail. I secretly hoped that when I pulled things from it during the frenzied breakfast rush, I missed a giant vat of pre-made soup. I opened the huge steel door. The cool refrigerated air swept over me, seeping into the kitchen. I stared at the multitude of shelves. Eggs, bacon, cheeses, bags of frozen vegetables; all things I had used and replaced this morning. Behind those stood eight containers labeled chicken broth.

"Well, it's a start." Racing through all the memories of the soups I'd watched designer chefs make on their cooking shows, I balanced the eight containers in my arms. They teetered precariously as I crossed the kitchen to the counter where the top two fell and landed with a thud. I set them all up-right and went back into the refrigerator. You could make almost any soup with a chicken broth base. The question was: what could I make, fast? Something I didn't have to simmer for hours to taste good. I rummaged through the frozen vegetables and came up with a large bag of sweet corn. A decent start.

I looked around for precooked chicken, but I couldn't find any. Well, chicken corn soup without chicken. And I glanced over at the bacon. That would make it tasty. I grabbed a slab of bacon and headed to the grill top.

Aerie rushed in. "Can you make a hamburger and French fries? Mr. Meyer, the bank manager, is here."

"No problem." I gave her a very forced grin. I could make this happen. I ran back to the refrigerator and seized the bag of beef patties and frozen French fries.

She quickly showed me how to work the deep fryer and I got to work dumping the fries into the basket and throwing two hamburgers on the grill. "Right." I told myself. "It helps if you turn it on." I fired up the gas grill.

"I can do this."

I pulled a huge pot from under the counter, rinsed it, and threw it on the stove top. I yanked the lids off the chicken broth containers and dumped them one by one into the pot. Only after the broth splashed over my shirt did I remember to put on an apron. Then I remembered that the chefs usually sauté onions first. I ran over and grabbed two onions from the produce bins and chopped them like crazy, saying a silent prayer that I wouldn't lose a finger. Once chopped I threw the onions onto the grill and they sizzled along with the hamburger. After flipping the hamburger, I realized the bacon needed to be on the grill as well.

Tearing open the packet of bacon was a challenge until I realized it was a peel-apart package. I sighed at myself and started to pull off slices. "There has to be a faster way to do this!"

Aerie walked in. "Is everything okay?"

"Everything is fine," I said through gritted teeth.

"Here, let me help you with that." Aerie took the bacon and peeled off strips like a pro and tossed them onto the griddle. You would never know she was a vegan.

I stirred the onions, flipped the burgers, and pulled a bun from the bag and tossed it face down on the griddle.

"Does he want lettuce or tomato?"

"Cheese and a slice of onion. And I have someone out there asking for soup."

"Ugh. The soup." I reached over and seized the bag of frozen corn, tore it open, and dumped it unceremoniously into the vat of chicken broth. With a spatula I scooped up the onions and threw them into the soup then flipped the bacon. I stirred the soup pot and turned up the gas.

It was time to plate the hamburger, so I grabbed a white plate from the shelf and snatched the bun from the grill.

I scooped up both patties and realized I had forgotten the cheese.

I put both patties back down on the grill, ran to the refrigerator, peeled a slice of cheese from the block, ran back, and threw it on top of one of the patties. I seized a cup of water and poured a couple tablespoons near the hamburgers and slammed a lid over it. In about twenty seconds the steam would melt the cheese. Sure enough, I lifted the lid and the cheese was gooey and melting down the sides of the burger. I scooped it up, slid it on the bun then ran to the cutting board and sliced a slab of onion and laid it on top of the other bun. And then I remembered...

"The fries!"

"I got them." Aerie ran over to the fryer and lowered the basket of fries. They sizzled and popped as they cooked.

"It'll only take four minutes. You can put the burger under the heat lamp." Aerie pointed to the counter between the kitchen and the dining room where a dark red heat lamp beamed down. "Take the onion off first," she recommended.

I did as I was told and went back to the soup.

The pot was just beginning to simmer, but it would be a few minutes before it was ready to serve.

I ran through the list of ingredients: chicken broth, corn, onion. The bacon! I glanced over at the grill. Thick plumes of smoke were rising from the bacon. I turned quickly from the soup pot and dragged the dishtowel too close to the burner. The burner that I had jacked up high so the soup would heat up faster. The dishtowel lit and flames licked at my face.

I screamed and dropped the towel to the floor and

stomped on it. A huge plume of bacon smoke rose gracefully above the grill and set off the fire alarm... and the sprinkler system.

For the second time in a week, I heard the wail of the fire siren.

13

Everyone emptied out onto the sidewalk. Aerie told the volunteer firemen that only some bacon and a dishtowel had burned. They made their way into the kitchen to make sure everything was okay.

As I stood outside and waited for them to return, I noticed Mr. Meyer, the bank manager, in a very heated conversation on his phone. I casually stepped in his direction, hoping he wouldn't notice.

"I understand, but I cannot allow you to open that box... Now let's not resort to vulgar threats." His face was sweaty and his hand holding the phone shook slightly.

Out of the corner of his eye he noticed me hovering, ended the phone call and slipped his cell phone into the breast pocket of his coat.

"I'm sorry you didn't get your burger." I hoped that would cover the fact I had been snooping. Maybe he'd think I'd been hovering simply to apologize.

"Good day, Ms. Michaels." He turned stiffly, walked across the street, and returned to the bank.

After helping Aerie clean up the kitchen, and after a

hundred apologies for almost burning down her diner, I told her what I had heard.

"Do you think it has anything to do with Becca or your house?"

"I'm not sure, but Mr. Meyer sounded like he was being threatened. It might be worth looking into."

Aerie appeared concerned.

"What's wrong?" I asked.

"I'll have to cancel my yoga class for tomorrow morning. I hate to do it, but the diner needs to open on time."

She turned towards me. "Unless..." She smiled at me.

"Unless what?"

"Unless you'd open it for me?"

"What? I almost burned down your diner. You'd trust me with the key?"

"I told you I can see auras...well, sometimes. I'm still figuring it out, but I can tell that you are very trustworthy. So yeah..." she reached into her pocket and pulled out a unicorn fob with a single key attached. "Here ya go."

I gave her a serious look. "I think you're crazy to give this to me." But I took the key anyway and stuffed it in my pocket. Unicorn and all.

THE NEXT MORNING, I opened the Soup and Scoop at 6 a.m. Robbie was still missing. I turned on the lights and the grill, started the coffee and decided right then and there that we weren't going to have a soup of the day on the menu today. Better no soup than another kitchen fire.

The bells on the door rang. I leaned out of the kitchen to see who had arrived. I watched as Mr. Meyer made his way to one of the stools at the counter.

"Can I help you, Mr. Meyer?"

"I'd like an egg sandwich and a cup of coffee, to go."

"Sure. No problem." This I could do without burning the place down. Hopefully.

As I put the English muffin in the toaster, Mr. Meyer leaned over the counter to peer in at me, concerned. "Where's Robbie?"

"Oh, he hasn't been in for a few days."

Mr. Meyer looked startled as he sat back on the stool. "As soon as it's ready, please. I need to get back to my office."

"No problem. I'll get it done as fast as I can." I planned to share his reaction with Aerie when she returned from yoga. I quickly put together the egg sandwich and poured him his cup of to-go coffee.

"Thank you, Ms. Michaels." He handed me a twenty and didn't even wait for his change before he was out the door.

Aerie arrived, still holding her yoga mat under her arm. She swept into the kitchen and placed her stuff near the aprons. She asked about Robbie, and I told her he hadn't shown up or called.

"I don't understand. This is just very out of character for him."

"Maybe we should talk to the chief about filing a missing person's report?"

Aerie looked worried. "Will you walk over with me after the breakfast rush?"

I nodded. "Sure. And I need to tell you about Mr. Meyer coming in here this morning."

I glanced around—the diner was slowly filling with customers. "Do you mind if I head over to the bank when it opens? I want to talk to Ellie and see what she can tell me about Mr. Meyer. When he learned that Robbie was missing, he seemed agitated more than upset."

"That's a great idea. We can ask her if she's seen Robbie at his house."

"Absolutely."

I helped her set up the tables, went back into the kitchen, and laid out the bacon and sausages.

The breakfast rush was relatively mild. It was easy for me to slip out and head toward the bank.

Seeing as it was on my way, I figured I should check my mailbox. I wasn't expecting much—I hadn't gotten around to notifying many people of my new PO box address. Mainly just the cell-phone people. Then it struck me as I walked into the post office. "Hi, Mike. Hey, do you know if Robbie has been in to pick up his mail lately?"

"Hey, Mira. No, he hasn't. His box is full. I was planning on pulling his mail and putting it together for him."

"I could take it to the diner, and we could store it there for him..."

"Sorry, I can only give his mail to the people listed on his PO box contract—I'll just hold if for him here."

I checked my own postbox; empty. I stepped away from the wall and scanned the boxes. It was easy to see which one was Robbie's. Multiple days' worth of junk mail pressed against the glass and filled the box.

"Bye, Mike. If I see Robbie, I'll let him know about his mail."

While I was bummed I couldn't check out Robbie's mail, I realized I had used the term 'we' when talking about the diner.

I had to be careful of putting down roots in relationships with guys—but I had to be careful of getting in too deep with Aerie and her cute diner too. A job that would help me pay to renovate the house. Perfect. A diner I started to think of as my home away from home. Problematic.

I MADE my way into the bank. As expected, Ellie sat there looking bored. When she saw me, she perked up. The girl loved gossip.

"Hey, Mira. I heard you guys had trouble at the diner yesterday. I saw the fire engine take off down the road. I'm pretty sure you made their day."

"Ha, ha. I burned the bacon and lit a towel on fire and it's kind of why I wanted to talk to you."

"Really?"

"Yeah, I'm cooking because Robbie hasn't shown up for work for the last two days, and I'm wondering if you'd seen him lately."

She thought for a moment. "No. I can't say that I have. Come to think of it, his truck wasn't in his driveway this morning."

"His mail is backed up too. Aerie and I are considering filing a missing person's report today with the chief."

"I hope he turns up. That's all we need is another murder in town."

Looking at her I wondered if that was exactly what she was hoping for; more gossip.

Now was as good a time as any to ask about Mr. Meyer. "Mr. Meyer came in for breakfast this morning and he had a strange reaction to Robbie being gone. Is anything going on with your boss?"

"He's having a rough week of it. I'll tell you that. A lot of people have been upset with him lately," she whispered. "I can't really talk here." She glanced at Mr. Meyer's closed office door. "But I can tell you what I found out about your house." She leaned forward like she had some juicy information.

Curiosity won the better of me and I moved closer. "What did you find?"

"As you know it was most recently sold to the town. Very recently, like right before you bought it."

"Okay?" I didn't think this was helpful. And she noticed my expression.

"But—" she let the word hang on the air— "I did find out that the paperwork for the previous owner has been blacked out with a marker."

"Really?"

"Yeah, obviously someone wants it to be kept a secret."

"And you don't know who lived in the house before me?"

"Like I said it's been empty for twenty years." Ellie herself was in her early twenties.

"Do you know anyone who would know?'

"I bet Mrs. Orsa would know. She's lived in this town forever."

Great. The old lady I keep bumping into. She had mentioned she was glad I had bought the house. Why? What did she know?

"You and Aerie are welcome to come by my place after work. I get off at four-thirty. We can take a look at Robbie's house together and see if he's there."

Just then Mr. Meyer stormed out of his office grumbling under his breath. When he saw Ellie leaning over the counter conspiratorially, he shouted, "Ms. Bracken, what have I told you about spreading gossip with the clientele?"

Ellie sat back and looked apologetic. "Sorry, Mr. Meyer." And then she grinned with the side of her mouth. "Have a nice afternoon, Ms. Michaels. I'll see you later." She looked right at Mr. Meyer when she said that.

I decided now was the best time for me to exit and I left

the bank. Ellie's exuberance for the dramatic scared me just a little.

FIVE O'CLOCK ROLLED AROUND QUICKLY. Aerie and I were seated in her kitchen recovering from a raging lunch rush. You'd think a kitchen fire would dissuade people from eating at the diner, but instead, it seemed like the whole town showed up. People kept craning their necks toward the kitchen, hoping to see some fire damage. Aerie gave up trying to calm people down—it was clear they wanted danger and gossip.

Aerie picked up our teacups and placed them in the sink.

"I'll drive," I suggested.

We stopped at my house to make sure Arnold was happy. He wasn't. Nothing major was amiss at my house though, so we hopped in the Buick, which miraculously started. I drove while Aerie gave directions. Robbie didn't live too far from downtown, but far enough that he couldn't walk to the Soup and Scoop. The place was a small rental property in a residential neighborhood, but in this town, I still considered it rural. There were only about six houses on this road.

Aerie pointed. "That's Ellie's house. And that would be Robbie's." I pulled up in front of his house, a low brown rancher with worn white trim. Robbie's truck wasn't parked there.

"He's not home. But I want to knock on the door anyway."

"I'd feel better if we checked." Aerie opened the car door

and got out. I followed her, and we stood on the sidewalk looking at Robbie's house, but not going any closer.

"Ellie says she doesn't remember seeing him recently. She seemed to want to tell me more but didn't want to talk at the bank."

"I think Mr. Meyer listens in on everything."

"Really?"

"Just a guess."

That would explain some things. "Ellie knows that he listens in on her, right?"

"She's the one who told me."

"Let's see what else she knows." We turned toward Ellie's house across the street.

Ellie had already opened her door and was walking down the front walk as we crossed the street. "I haven't seen anything since I got home, but that was only half an hour ago. Should we go over?" Ellie was already halfway across the street.

"Hey, Ellie, I'm sorry if I got you into trouble with Mr. Meyer today."

"Don't worry about it. He was bound to blow at some point. Everyone has been yelling at him today." Ellie strode up to Robbie's house. Over her shoulder, she called out, "I can handle Mr. Meyer." I exchanged glances with Aerie. I'd love to know why everyone was yelling at the bank manager. Aerie shrugged. We turned our attention back to Ellie, who appeared to be taking measures into her own hands.

"She's knocking on his door!" We ran to catch up.

The three of us crowded together on the front stoop. No sound or movement came from inside. I knocked on the glass storm door. Ellie elbowed me gently, took out a pair of gloves, and slipped them on her hands. "We don't necessarily want anyone to know we've been here. Right?"

She smiled sweetly. Aerie and I stepped back, not knowing what Ellie had planned.

She turned the storm door handle, pulled it open, and reached for the front doorknob. I wanted to stop her because breaking and entering wasn't my thing. On the other hand, if something had happened to Robbie, we needed to try and help. My instinct to help overruled my impulse to not break the law. I stayed silent.

Ellie turned the knob and pushed. Locked. She turned her slight body and rammed her shoulder into the door.

"Ellie!?" Aerie and I whispered loudly.

"What? We want to find out, don't we?" She closed the storm door. "It won't open anyway." She shrugged.

"Let's go around back," I said. "Maybe we'll find something there." Mostly I just wanted to get Ellie out of the public eye. There weren't a ton of houses here, but who knows who was peering out windows or would happen to drive past. If Ellie did something rash, and anyone saw my car here, it would be pinned on me—like I needed any more reasons to deal with the police.

"I'll go around this way, you two go that way," Ellie suggested.

When she walked away, I leaned toward Aerie. "Go with her, just in case. We don't need to have one of the other neighbors call the police if she decides to break and enter."

Aerie nodded and followed Ellie.

I scanned the outside of the house as I walked toward the backyard. All the windows were closed, and the blinds pulled shut. Everything inside was dark. The house stood silent.

When I got to the backyard, I found Ellie holding the screen door for Aerie who pounded on the back door.

"Robbie! Are you in there?" she shouted. I looked around, and I relaxed a tiny bit, no one could see us here.

A chain rattled and then a loud bark came from the other side of the door.

Robbie had a dog. And from the sounds of it, a big dog. The chain rattled again, and the back door shook with each bark. Dog claws dragged down the other side of the wooden door.

Ellie stepped back, frightened by the intensity of the noise.

Aerie grabbed the doorknob and yanked. "Oh, the poor baby. What if no one has fed him?"

"It sounds like he's chained up inside," I said.

After yanking on the door in a futile attempt, I looked up the number for the ASPCA. But when I told them the situation, they reminded me they were two towns over and wouldn't be able to get there for hours.

Ellie eyed the door. "I'm a bit afraid of whatever is on the other side of this, but if you guys want, I can show you how to take the hinges off to get in."

I raised an eyebrow and looked at Aerie who stifled a grin. "You know what, Ellie," I said. "Thanks for all your help but it's okay, you can head home. We'll go to the police station and have someone come out here and open the door.

The dog let out a low whine. Aerie looked pained.

"We should go," I said.

"Okay, if you guys need me though, you know where I live." Ellie looked sad to see the excitement end.

"Thanks again, Ellie, for everything." She accompanied us back to my car.

"See you guys later." Ellie walked over to her house and Aerie and I watched as she went in and closed the door.

"Well, I know who to call when I'm in the mood for a good break-in."

Aerie nodded. "Was there more we wanted to ask her about Mr. Meyer?"

"I definitely wanted to pick her brain more. But information isn't worth us getting arrested for Ellie's compulsion for breaking and entering."

As if on cue, the police chief's car turned onto the street.

"Oh, Mira, see if you can flag him down and we can get this poor puppy some food."

"Right." I ran out to the street and waved, but he either didn't see me, or was on his way to something important.

"That's okay. We can get Dan over here to let that poor dog out." Aerie was determined. I drove quickly toward downtown thinking if I disappeared, what would happen to poor Arnold trapped in the house and unable to get his own food and water.

14

By the time we got to the station, we were both more than a little panicky about the poor dog. Detective Lockheart sat at his desk typing away at his keyboard. He sat, plain as day, behind the woman at the counter who refused to let me back there.

"Can I just talk to him, please?" I pleaded.

She put her hands on the desk between us. "Not right now, he's working on a case."

"It's probably a case that involves my house. We have something that is even more pressing right now." Again, I imagined Arnold howling behind my front door, alone, with no one to hear or help him.

She rolled her eyes at me. "Fine, I'll let him know you're here." She swiveled in her chair. "Dan," she yelled as if he was in a different zip code, not four feet away. "These women say they have something important to discuss!" She turned back to the papers on her desk, ignoring us.

Detective Lockheart didn't look up. In fact, he continued staring at the computer screen as if we weren't there. As if that woman hadn't yelled anything at him.

Aerie edged past the woman and up to Detective Lockheart's desk. "Dan, we need your help to get into Robbie's house. A dog is in there, we haven't seen Robbie in two days, and we think his dog may need to be fed."

He continued to type. "Did you call the ASPCA?"

I joined Aerie. "Yes, but they don't know when they can make it out here."

"I'm in the middle of an actual investigation. I don't have time to go feed a dog." He glared at the back of the woman who didn't stop us from getting to his desk.

Aerie leaned in between him and his laptop. "You won't take time out of your day to help some poor defenseless animal who might be starving and dehydrated?" Her words dripped with indignation.

He looked up at Aerie. "I didn't say I wouldn't help." He pushed away from his desk. "I just said that I am busy working on an actual investigation. I can't take time out of my day for every whim that comes along."

While we had his attention I continued, "Look, Detective. This won't take much of your time. We just need you to open the door so we can check on the wellness of Robbie's animal, and we would like to open a missing person's report for Robbie because he has not been to work in two days. Either something bad has happened to him or he deliberately left his dog behind."

"And you don't want me telling everyone about your negligence to animals," Aerie added.

"You know what? Fine." He took a step away from the desk. "We'll head over to Robbie's house and we will check on his dog. And after that you both promise me you will leave me alone?"

"Absolutely. We will leave you completely alone." Aerie smiled.

"We don't want to bother you in any way anymore. You can work on your investigation in peace," I added.

IT DIDN'T TAKE MUCH MORE than fifteen minutes to get back over to Robbie's house. We stood outside my car and in the front lawn while Detective Dan got something out of his police car glove box. Aerie folded her arms across her chest. "Why would Robbie leave his dog behind?"

"Maybe someone threatened him. He did have that black-eye the other day."

"He said he had errands to run before he left that day."

"And we haven't seen him since." She trembled with concern. Aerie was loyal to her friends.

Detective Lockheart gave us both a stern look. "You shouldn't have taken it upon yourselves to come here."

"Detective, we just knocked on his door to see if he was home."

"If it has been forty-eight hours, like you say, then you can place a missing person's report and we can investigate properly," he reprimanded.

Aerie jumped in. "How long would it take you to come to Robbie's house? His poor dog has been there for what could be days, without any food."

We walked around the back of the house. Detective Lockheart held a pen shaped item in his hand.

"What is that?" I asked.

"Something that will help me break a pane of glass if I need to."

"You will help us get to the dog?"

He picked up his pace and we walked around the back of the house.

I pulled open the screen door and grabbed the knob expecting it to be locked but it released easily, and I pushed it open. A medium-size short-haired terrier bounded out and Aerie grabbed him by the collar. I took a closer look, this door had definitely been locked.

"Hey, little guy." He licked her face. Aerie stroked his head.

Dan pocketed his glass-breaking pen, stepped inside the kitchen, and looked around. I followed him. A bag of dog food sat next to a full dish in the corner of the kitchen near the door.

Dan pointed to the dish. "Obviously, he is feeding his dog...or someone else is."

Dan walked further into the kitchen toward the living room at the front of the house. "I don't see anything suspicious. Maybe Robbie simply had plans and he didn't want to share them with you. Did that occur to either of you?"

"He didn't give us any indication that he planned to leave town. And he did have a black eye."

"A fight. He probably had issues and went to visit family, and I know for a fact his family lives in the city." Dan headed toward the open door. "I have to get back to a serious investigation." He looked at me. "When Robbie feels he needs to let you know what's going on in his life, I'm sure you'll see him again. Right now, I don't have any reason to put a missing person's report out on him. Now, if you excuse me."

Dan ushered me out of the house. "Miss McIntyre, I think it's safe to leave Robbie's dog here. Obviously, someone is feeding him."

Aerie reluctantly brought the dog back inside. But then I

changed my mind. "We should really see to it that Robbie's pet is properly taken care of while he's gone."

Dan looked at me like I was crazy.

"Mira is right, we don't know if he's getting enough outdoor time while Robbie is away. We have a responsibility to make sure this dog gets the proper attention."

"I don't want some sort of issue later when he gets back and finds his dog missing." Dan eyed the two of us suspiciously.

"We'll leave a note to let him know we're taking care of his dog and that he can come by at any time to pick him up," Aerie rambled as she snuggled the little dog to her chest.

"Fine, fine. Hurry up. I have work to do."

Aerie held the dog close while I went back inside to get the bag of dog food and leash. One of Robbie's kitchen drawers hung open. Everything inside was jumbled. Robbie kept a pristine kitchen at the Soup and Scoop. It was odd that he'd leave a drawer open, let alone one that was completely disorganized.

"I don't have all day." The detective tapped his foot.

"Coming." I reluctantly exited the house.

Dan engaged the doorknob lock and pulled the door closed.

"What about the open door?" Aerie took the leash from me and clicked it onto the dog's collar.

"When Aerie and I were here earlier, this door was definitely locked. Otherwise we would have never had to bother you to help us save the dog."

"This dog never needed saving. Whoever is feeding the dog accidentally left the door open. It's not a crime. Actually, in a small town like this, most people leave the back door open." He quickened his pace as he headed toward his car.

"Remember, you promised—no more bothering me at work. And let me do the investigating in this town, Ms. Michaels." He got in his rundown Chevy and drove off.

Once the bag of dog food was in the backseat, we were ready to go. Aerie held the pup in her lap while I started the car. Or tried to start the car.

"Come on." I turned the key and on the third try the engine turned over. "Phew."

"It's done that before?"

"Yeah, she's old, but she still gets me from point A to point B. Most of the time."

"You know we have a good mechanic up the street from you."

"Yeah? Well, maybe I'll take her in." Although the last thing I wanted to do was spend more money on the car.

She tickled the dog under his chin, and he responded by licking her hand and then her face. "Such a cute little thing," Aerie cooed.

"He looks like a light brown miniature Toto." He let out a small woof.

Aerie turned the pup around. "Oops, sorry, honey. She's a she."

"Toto still works."

"Let's go back to my place and I'll figure out something for dinner."

"I can cook if you want. I miss having my own kitchen."

"Jay told me he is still going to help you fix your kitchen, even though...you know."

I nodded. "I feel so bad about everything I said." I doubted Jay would ever forgive me. He told me he'd keep his word and help, but he hadn't mentioned anything about forgiving me. "It would be nice to have a kitchen again.

Actually, it would be nice to have a house that's solid on all four sides."

When we got back to Aerie's house, I made us tomato soup from a can, and grilled cheese sandwiches for our dinner. "What do you think her name is?"

"Robbie mentioned her once, but I don't think he told me her name."

Aerie had poured a bowl of dog food for our little Toto and the sound brought out her cat. At the sight of the dog, the cat hissed, charged Toto with claws flailing until the pup scampered whining behind my legs.

Aerie quickly picked up Snowball and took her into the next room, then closed the door.

"I can take Toto for the night," I told Aerie. "I don't think Arnold would mind as much." I knew I could talk him into it, or at least try to.

"Thanks. I feel bad. She's such a sweet thing. I don't want her to be terrorized by Snowball."

We sat eating our dinner which reminded me of Saturday afternoons as a kid. I even dunked my sandwich into my soup.

"You know right before we left Robbie's house, I noticed that one of the kitchen drawers was open."

"Yeah?"

"Well, what was odd is that everything inside was mixed up like it had been rummaged through."

"That's not like Robbie. He's highly organized in the kitchen. Do you think somebody could have been in his house?"

"I believe someone has been there, probably while we were in town. Why else was the door unlocked when we came back with Detective Lockheart?" I tossed back the last bite of my sandwich. "Do you have a piece of paper and maybe a pen?"

"Sure." Aerie opened what could only have been a junk drawer and searched until she pulled out a small pad of paper and a ballpoint.

"Thanks. I want to make a list of all the stuff that's been going on. Maybe that way we can make sense of it all."

"Number one was Becca's murder. She was found in the kitchen of my house. And it looked like she had been hit in the head with the leg of a chair and the broken chair was left in my kitchen. The kitchen was later set on fire."

"When I was finally allowed back into the house, it smelled horrible, like disinfectant. Then, that same night, I woke up and got out of the house before the fire, so whatever clues were in there were burned to ashes."

"You smelled the fire?"

I couldn't bring myself to tell her about the ghost or that Arnold had woken me.

"Yeah, I guess so. That's when I saw Jay outside."

"I did send him over to check on you that night. Everything about you going back to your house that night felt wrong. I'm glad he was there. I don't even want to think about what could have happened if you had been asleep and Jay hadn't been there."

"I'm fine, but my kitchen is not. If it was done on purpose, they knew what they were doing because when Jay and I cleaned it up there wasn't much left. We threw out most of the glass and damaged wood, including most of the roof."

"Jay had said the front window was locked when we left you, but after the fire it was found open."

"Right, open but broken. Whoever set the fire got in that way."

"Do you think someone set the fire to stop you from asking questions about Becca's murder?"

"It won't work. I don't scare that easily. And I can feel it. We're close to figuring this out. What about Becca's dad?"

Aerie nodded. "He's had his problems. That's for sure."

"People at the diner mentioned that he was recently seen in town."

"Do you think maybe something happened and he got violent with Becca?"

I nodded and added his name to the list.

"Robbie came in with a black eye and disappeared after that," Aerie added. "And then you overheard Mr. Meyer on the phone the day of the grill fire."

I wrote it down. "When I talked with Ellie, she mentioned something about Mr. Meyer having a hard time with someone."

Aerie held Toto and rubbed behind her ears.

"Do we know why Becca's car was still parked at the realtor office when she was found at my house?"

"No. Chelsea said somebody must've met her at the office and they drove her to your house."

"So, whoever picked her up at the office could be the killer."

"Unless somebody took her to the house and left, and then someone else met her there and killed her."

"Do we know if it was Jay? I mean, not the killer, not the killer." I looked up at Aerie afraid she might think I was accusing her brother again. "I mean if he picked her up at the office and drove her to my house. Otherwise we can assume whoever picked her up, she knew."

"What about Chelsea? I mean she automatically gets a promotion once Becca is out of the picture."

"If she's the murderer that would keep my brother from dating her, I'd hope."

"She's a suspect." I wrote her name and her motive. It was easy to do; we both disliked Chelsea.

"Do you think Jay took Becca to my house?"

"I can ask him if he comes home."

"He hasn't come home?"

"No. He's still mad at me." She shrugged sadly.

"I'm so sorry, Aerie."

She snuggled the dog. "It's not your fault. Sure, he's mad we suggested he could have had a role in Becca's death. But I only thought that because he has been so weird with me the last few weeks. He was basically keeping things from me. I'm furious that he's dating Chelsea, and that he wouldn't talk to me about wanting to move out." She sighed.

"You guys are close—you'll get through this."

I drank the last of my tomato soup from the bowl while I mulled over everything that we knew. "Do you think the bank manager had anything to do with it?"

"Do you think so?"

"I did hear Mr. Meyer's side of a threatening phone conversation." I wrote his name on our list. "What kind of box would Mr. Meyer and Becca have access to that would get her killed and him threatened?"

"That's a good question."

"Ellie seemed kind of suspicious about the situation and she was definitely a bit overzealous with the breaking and entering."

Aerie almost snarfed her tomato soup. "Ellie would love to be a secret spy and know all the town's secrets."

We giggled. It felt good to laugh. "I'll stop by the bank tomorrow and see what I can find out. I can ask her to see what she can learn about her boss and the closed-door meetings he's been having lately."

Aerie nodded. "That's a good idea."

After cleaning up we called it a day.

I picked up Toto and snuggled her under my arm and brought her out to my car to take her home. Up the street toward my house I saw detective Lockheart's white Chevy pulling away.

"Aerie, come out here."

She rushed to my side. "What is it?"

"Dan Lockheart just left my house."

"I'll come with you."

"No. I'm sure it's fine. But I am wondering what he's up to." I was exhausted and feeling the need to be alone after the hectic day.

Aerie seemed to understand. "You have my cell number. Call me when you get home."

"Thanks, Aerie. See you tomorrow." I gave her a quick hug.

Hopefully Arnold wouldn't mind that I was bringing another pet home for the night. Considering he was so concerned with preserving his territory, I hoped he wouldn't cause too much drama. I sighed. Was it too much to ask for one quiet night at home without bickering pets, ghosts, explosions, or a murder?

15

I had Toto tucked under my arm while I unlocked the front door. She licked my face and I giggled. But the smile melted off my face as I stepped inside of my house. Someone had broken in and ransacked everything. The house was a disaster.

"Arnold? Buddy, where are you?" I tried to keep my voice calm, but hysteria crept in. "Arnold!"

I put Toto down and ran through the dining room toward the kitchen, thinking they had broken in through there, and maybe Arnold had gotten out, but the plywood Jay had hammered in place held firm against the wall. I stood very still and listened. The house seemed to be holding its breath. Except for the padding of Arnold's feet as he came into the dining room and greeted me with a headbutt to my shins. "Arnold! You answer me when I call you." I cuddled him, relieved he was okay. But was he? I held him at arm's length to inspect him. His claws were ragged. "What happened here, buddy?" He meowed back.

I couldn't calm my mind enough to "listen" to Arnold.

I pressed the power on my cell phone. Dead. I had forgotten to charge it, again.

I walked through the house holding Arnold, trailed by Toto. The folding chairs in the dining room lay on their backs. The dusty curtains puddled on the floor. I was suddenly thankful for the fact that I owned very little. Nothing appeared to be missing. I hadn't left any money behind. I hadn't brought any valuables with me when I moved. So why would someone break into my house? What were they looking for?

I turned on the lights as I moved, but I grabbed the flashlight from the table and put Arnold down to hold the flashlight backwards—a better weapon than the yoga mat. I tiptoed up the stairs. The steepest and longest staircase of my life. At the top, I listened again, sounds from outside. Crickets. A window was open up here. Both animals followed me on my inspection of the house. Arnold wasn't even asking me about our new guest—it seemed we were all too upset to communicate anything.

The outside sounds came from the master bedroom. I flipped on the lights and brandished my flashlight. Walking around the room, I kept my back to the wall, until I got to the window. I peered out. Nothing. No ladder, but obviously somebody used one to get up here. This had to be how they broke in. There wasn't much to this room, no furniture, yet the closet door stood open. Whoever had been in here had been searching for something.

I didn't want to see my own room. The violation of some stranger having gone through my stuff already made my ears burn and my heart race. Anger lit up every cell in my body. But I forced myself to walk down the hallway and look.

I opened the door to my room. I flipped on the light and

took a quick glance and confirmed the train-wreck-mess that would have to be cleaned up. I didn't bother to go in. I was too angry. I charged down the hallway and checked the other rooms and the bathroom. They had hit every single room. What could they possibly be looking for? At the end of the hallway the attic door stood open.

I slowly crept down the hall towards the open door, listening intently. But the only thing I heard were my own footsteps. Arnold walked by my side. I took one last listen at the base of the attic stairs. Nothing but the normal creaks of the house.

We made our way upstairs. The attic floor and walls gave off a warm heated wood smell. A dusty, but pleasant scent. I glanced around the open space. Aerie had said the attic was huge, and it was. The entire floor plan of the house lay before me, only without walls to divide it up. Open from one end to the other. A single naked light bulb dangled from the center beam casting bright light on the stairs, shadowing the corners in darkness.

Whoever had broken in had been more systematic up here with their search. Things have been moved, but not tossed. Against one wall stood a series of shelves, and next to them on the floor sat a large antique wooden chest embedded with a brass lock. I had never seen anything like it before. It was beautiful and mysterious and ancient, and it dominated the entire area.

The dust on the floor near the chest was disturbed by a number of footprints. The chest itself was slightly askew from the shelves, as if someone had tried to pick it up but it had been too heavy. I flipped my flashlight over and turned it on and shone the light into the corner and saw more footprints. A clue for sure. They looked like the impression of a man's work boot. Definitely not a woman's shoe. Not

Aerie's small delicate foot or the sandals she generally wore. I turned back, making sure that Arnold and Toto stayed away from the footprints. I had to assume that some of them, at least, were from the intruder. Who had been up here? And why?

Arnold rubbed against my leg. I sat down on the dusty floor next to him. "Who was it? Who was in the house?"

All I know is someone came into my territory without proper authority from either you or me, so I showed him the paw and the claw. And I believe I got a bite in for good measure, but he was much larger than a cat, so I was overpowered.

"Who was it?"

I think it was a human.

"That's not helpful Arnold."

Possibly male because of his scent. I do remember his foot pads. Because it was the last thing I could see before he moved off into the house.

"His shoes?"

Yes, those things.

I sighed. The footprints in front of me could tell me that. "You said he knocked you out?"

Battle wounds, nothing important.

Toto whined.

I stood and brushed the dust from my pants. I needed to get Arnold to a vet, but I wasn't telling him that or he'd hide in some unreachable corner.

As we walked down the stairs from the attic, I noticed that he favored his front paw. Aerie would know the vet. My cell phone was still dead, and although I hated admitting it, I needed some company.

After I gingerly placed Arnold into the carrier, I picked up Toto, and we headed for the car. My car seemed to know

I was already on the edge and started right away. We drove the short distance to Aerie's.

I was shaking by the time I got there.

She was livid. "I told you I should have come over with you." She paced the kitchen floor. "What if the person was still in your house? You could have been the next one." She shivered at the thought.

"I'm okay, Aerie. Seriously." Letting her express some of the feelings I was trying to push down and not feel was actually cathartic. "Whoever broke into my house was looking for something. And they weren't there when I got home."

Snowball entered the kitchen and howled at Toto. Aerie picked her up and carried her into the other room and closed the door.

"Do you remember seeing Dan as I was leaving?" I needed to know what she thought.

"Dan wouldn't break in. He's a cop. He just wouldn't do that; I've known him too long."

"Whoever it was, it looks like Arnold got in a few good swipes before they left. I really want to take him to the vet and have him checked out."

"Of course. I'll drive." She grabbed her car keys from the peg near the door.

I swallowed, relieved at her offer. I was feeling shaky again. What if Arnold had been seriously hurt?

BY THE TIME we got to the vet's office Arnold was growling in his carrier and Toto had peed on me. She obviously enjoyed car rides, to an extreme. Dealing with the normal-every-day kind of insanity that was having pets distracted me from the reality of the past few hours, in a good way.

"I have to get cleaned up." I focused on the ridiculousness of being covered in dog pee and not wanting to touch anything.

"I can take Arnold and Toto and let them know we're here. You go ahead and wash up." She snickered.

"Next time you get to hold Toto."

"Right." She winked.

I went to the bathrooms located next to the front door of the vet's office. Washing my hands and cleaning my clothes helped me think logically again.

Who would break into my house? And why had Detective Lockheart knocked on my door? My car was just a few houses away—if he had needed to ask me something, one glance up the street would have told him where I was. He couldn't have been looking for clues. Any evidence to Becca's death was either already in police custody or had burned in the fire. And what was so important about the attic? What were they looking for? If it was a previous owner wanting their attic junk back, all they'd have to do was ask. None of this made sense.

I washed up as best I could with hand soap and thin paper towels and headed into the waiting room.

Aerie was no longer there. They must've called her into the back room with the animals.

Someone was behind the desk in the far corner, having a heated, and by the way he turned his body, private, phone conversation. The ID tag on his jacket labeled him the vet.

"No, Dad, he can't make you open the safety deposit box. Don't let him pressure you." He paused and added, "Don't let him bully you. If it gets worse call Uncle Jack. He's a lawyer."

I opened the door to the back area and looked left and

right for Aerie. I followed the sound of yapping dog. Sure enough, I found them.

The vet assistant had Arnold by the scruff while petting and cooing at him. She looked up when I came in. "Hi, I'm Bonnie the vet assistant." She shook my hand. "I just finished getting his vitals, and I'll have Dr. Meyer take a look at Arnold here."

I raised an eyebrow. Dr. Meyer? "Thank you," I said as she walked out. Then I grabbed Aerie's arm and whispered in her ear. "Is Dr. Meyer related to Mr. Meyer the bank manager?"

"Yes, I think he is Dr. Meyers father."

I nodded. "I heard an interesting conversation..."

With a quick knock at the door, Dr. Meyer walked into the room.

I smiled obnoxiously. "Hi, Dr. Meyer." He gave me a quick glance that told me he thought I was crazy. Just as long as he hadn't heard what I was saying.

"Well, let's take a look at Arnold here. He held Arnold by the scruff turned him around to examine his paws. "Bonnie mentioned there was an altercation?" I glanced at Aerie. She shrugged.

"Right. He had a bit of a fight." I shifted my weight onto my other foot. "I just wanted to have him checked out to make sure he's okay. Because, we didn't see it happen."

Dr. Meyer nodded without looking up. After examining Arnold's ribs and claws, he nodded. "He appears to be fine. A broken claw or two." He took out a pair of trimmers and clipped the rough edges. "I'm sure whoever was on the receiving end probably has a few souvenirs."

He cleaned up Arnold's paws with a cotton pad dipped in rubbing alcohol. When he finished, he balled it up and threw it into a trashcan under the counter. "He should be fine. But if you see any changes in behavior, we'd certainly like to see him again. You can check out with Bonnie at the front desk." His cell phone rang.

"Thank you, Dr. Meyer." I wondered if it was his father again.

Dr. Meyer ducked out quickly. I handed Toto to Aerie, went back to the trashcan, snatched up the alcohol swabs, and stuffed them into my pocket. There could be DNA from whomever had been in my house. I could send it to friends of Darla's in Boston. I was going to find out who did this.

16

I awoke having barely slept. I hoped one day I'd be able to
sleep soundly in this house. When the murder was
resolved, and people stopped breaking in...maybe then I'd
sleep, so long as the ghost kept her singing to herself.

I laughed out loud, startling both Arnold on my pillow
and Toto from her spot at the foot of my bed. This was my
big adventure. I was just supposed to flip a house, make
some money, and get on with my life. But now I was
sequestering myself and two animals in my small guest
room, worried that the person who ransacked my house
would come back. Not to mention that I was embroiled in
the murder investigation and couldn't find my way out.

Maybe I should have taken Aerie up on her offer to sleep
at her place—I'd probably have gotten more sleep. But I also
wanted to prove to myself that I could do this on my own.
She had taken the unicorn key back from me and told me to
sleep in—that she would open the diner.

I un-barricaded the door and tried to get some answers
from Arnold. But he wasn't terribly coherent and said he

just wanted to sleep. He also finally had some choice words about me taking in any stray off the street. I took Toto for a quick jaunt around the yard.

During the night of broken sleep, I had convinced myself that Detective Dan was the one who ransacked my house. Watching his Chevy pull away from my property, he became suspect number one in my mind. I headed over to the police station to share a word or two with him. My place may have been a crime scene, but it wasn't any longer and I deserved my privacy. What gave him the right to break into my house and invade my personal space.

By the time I opened the door to the station, I was livid. I walked straight up to the woman who was extremely unhelpful the first time I'd been there. "I'd like to talk to Dan Lockheart, please."

She gave me the side eye but, surprisingly, said, "If you'd like to have a seat, I'll get him for you."

Before I could even get over my surprise the detective was at my side, shaking my hand. "I'm glad you could come in."

"You're expecting me?" What nerve this guy had.

"I left a note on your front door."

"You call that a note? Well you certainly let me know that you were there."

"You didn't get it?" He took his hand back and looked me over.

"Weren't you the one that ransacked every single room in my house—and what the heck is so important in my attic?"

The detective raised both palms, fending off my bitter assault. "Whoa. I didn't break into your house."

"I saw your car on the street in front of my house yesterday. Right before I came home to find my house a mess."

"Let's have this conversation in a conference room." He ushered me to a small glass-sided room with a desk and four chairs. I reluctantly sat down. I really didn't want to hear his excuses.

"I came by your house last night because I was wondering if I could interview you again. I need more information about what you witnessed when you arrived at your house and found Becca. I also need to learn more about the possible cause of the fire. I left multiple messages on your cell phone, which kept going straight to voicemail. I thought maybe it had been damaged in the fire and you weren't getting my messages."

I ignored the thing about my cell phone; I was tired of my sister's million messages, so I stopped listening to them. Forgetting to charge it was par for the course with me. Still, I couldn't believe his nerve. "You don't have enough evidence from the multiple days you spent inside my house?"

He looked down at his hands. "No." He looked up again, "Did you file a report for the break-in?"

"That's why I'm here, duh." He made me so frustrated. But he was also looking less and less like a suspect.

Detective Lockheart pulled a legal pad from a cabinet. "The break-in had to have happened before I arrived. I didn't notice anything amiss from the front of the house."

"They came in through an upstairs window. It was wide open. They must've used a ladder."

The detective made notes. "Did you touch anything?"

"It's my house. I cleaned up so I could go to bed."

He made more notes and a clicking sound with his tongue. "You probably destroyed evidence."

"If you still need to talk to me about the reason for the murder and the fire, you obviously don't have a good track record with evidence."

"I'm not the reason evidence is missing." He stood abruptly and took a deep breath. "Never mind that."

"What do you mean? What's missing?"

"It's not your concern."

"This whole thing is my concern. I can't seem to live in my own house. Things keep happening. Not little things, either!" It was definitely the sleep deprivation talking. "Since I've been here, someone's been murdered. Then someone blew up the crime scene and burned down my kitchen. After that someone climbed into a top floor window in broad daylight and ransacked my entire house! There hasn't been a day when I haven't had to clean up from a murder, a fire, or an intruder. And on top of all of this crazy there's the ghost." It slipped out. I had said it. The ghost.

The detective stared at me. Noticing how tired I was, he grinned. "For all that, I'm really sorry."

"You should be. I don't want to be in the middle of all this." I stood up. This interview was over and the sooner I could get out of here the better.

Detective Lockheart cleared his throat. "We found Robbie's truck abandoned outside of town."

"Abandoned?" I sat back down.

"It looks like it. There's nothing inside the cab. The truck is empty."

"So, what happened to him?"

"We were hoping you or Aerie might know more."

"The last time we heard from Robbie was two days before we talked to you."

The detective stood and paced. For the first time I noticed he looked tired, worn out. "Thank you for coming by today, Ms. Michaels. I'll have one of the officers take a more formal statement regarding the break-in." He waved an arm towards the door. "And I'd like to come with you to your house and review whatever evidence is left behind."

"Fine. But I'm staying in my house."

After filling out a ton of paperwork and talking to the officer about the break-in, I looked around for Detective Dan. I didn't see him anywhere. He had said he'd come home with me, and I would probably feel better if someone in an official capacity looked over things. But clearly, something more important than me had come up. I was tired of feeling like I was always waiting around for the police. In fact, I refused to wait around anymore. I jammed my phone in my back pocket and headed out the door.

I walked past the alleyway next to the police station. Someone called my name. The detective must have seen me leave. I planned to give him another piece of my mind for making me wait. I came around the corner of the building into the parking lot and was slammed into the brick wall, an arm pressed against my throat. Stars peppered my sight. I choked to catch my breath. I blinked my eyes open only to see a man wearing a black ski mask.

"Where is the key?" his gravelly voice whispered into my ear.

I squirmed against the iron bar of his arm against my neck. "What key?" came out in a breathless whisper.

"I know Robbie gave it to you. Where is it?"

I reached my arms up to push his elbow out of my throat, but it was like concrete. I looked down at his shoes and brought my knee up fast and hard.

Immediately the vice grip on my neck ceased. He doubled over and coughed. I ran.

I ran toward that stupid house which had been nothing

but grief to me. I couldn't understand why I didn't just walk back into the police station. I wanted to get as far away from the altercation as possible. By the time I got to my front door some semblance of common sense came to me. I took a deep breath and I headed over to the Soup and Scoop. I needed to talk to Aerie.

17

I opened the door to the diner and bumped into Aerie. I pulled her aside before blurting out my crazy thought. "I think Detective Lockheart just tried to strangle me."

"What? You're kidding." She walked with me to the kitchen. "Sit down, you're shaking."

I sat on the crates next to the refrigerator. "Not kidding. I was at the police station and I talked to him, but he disappeared while I gave my statement of the break-in to another officer."

Aerie handed me a glass of water.

My throat hurt as I sipped. "He said he wanted to take a look at my house, when I couldn't find him, I left. Someone called my name from the parking lot behind the station. So, I followed the voice." I closed my eyes to gather myself. "Whoever it was, the detective or someone else, pushed me against the building and strangled me." I tentatively touched the back of my head.

Aerie took one look at my head and stuffed some ice into a bag for my bruise.

"Thanks. I gave him a solid knee to the crotch."

"I'm calling Jay."

"Why?"

"He's friends with Dan."

"No." I tried to stand but my head felt like it weighed two hundred pounds. I sat back down. "No. Jay won't believe me. Not after everything that has happened."

"I'm worried. Things are getting more dangerous. And when I need help—" Aerie shrugged— "I ask my big brother."

I nodded. Maybe it would help Aerie mend the rift between her and Jay.

I sat nursing the lump on the back of my head and the pressure that I still felt over my throat. The longer I sat, the angrier I got. I should just pick up everything and move, but I couldn't go back home. I had no money anyway. I wasn't about to let some jerk force me to do anything. I was determined to figure this out.

When Jay stepped through the back door Aerie grabbed him by the arm and hustled him into the kitchen. "Tell him what happened," she said to me.

"Mira, are you okay?!" Jay carefully lifted the second bag of ice off the back of my head and inspected my bump. My sleep-deprived, addled mind wanted him to lean closer.

Because he had a girlfriend, and it wasn't me, I took a deep breath and strengthened my resolve. "I'm okay. I promise."

I started to recount everything, but I guess I was too slow. Aerie filled him in with one exceptionally long sentence.

Jay nodded. "You're sure it was Dan?"

"He had a balaclava-like mask on his face."

"You didn't see anyone else around? Did you recognize his voice?" Jay asked.

I shook my head. "We were alone. And he spoke low and gravelly. Disguising it."

"Why didn't you go back into the police station?"

Aerie punched him in the arm. "Because she was scared. She ran here."

"I felt safer here. Whoever it was wants some kind of key that they think I have." I tried to remember what the attacker had said to me. But I couldn't make my brain replay the incident. Self-preservation, I guessed. "Something about Robbie giving it to me."

Aerie looked at Jay. "Do you think he had anything to do with Robbie's disappearance?"

Jay shook his head. "Look, I don't think it was Dan."

"How do you know? He could be hiding it from you." Aerie glared at him.

"I don't think so. He's been really frustrated with this case."

"Yeah, because he's trying to cover up everything."

"No, he's frustrated because the evidence keeps going missing. The fire destroyed a good part of what they needed to review for Becca's death. And the chief sent her body to the city for the autopsy and Dan hasn't been able to get a hold of the results."

"Okay," Aerie started. "Let's say it's not Dan. Who could it be?"

"If it's not Dan. It still has to be someone Robbie knows, and someone that Becca knows."

They both nodded.

"But who?"

I mentally checked off our list of suspects, but Robbie and Becca knew all of them.

Aerie and I waited at the diner while Jay went down to the police station to find and bring back the detective.

I physically flinched when Detective Lockheart came into the diner. Aerie saw it. "You still think it was him?"

I shook my head. "I don't know. My head hurts, my throat is sore, and I'm an emotional mess."

"Just stay here." Aerie strode into the dining room.

She spoke with Detective Lockheart and Jay. Detective Lockheart glanced up at me with a pained expression.

It was then that I realized it couldn't have been him. Besides his expression, I realized he was taller than the guy who grabbed me. I let out a breath. At least whoever was after me wasn't legally allowed to carry a gun.

Oh, who was I kidding? If someone was bent on murder, the choice of weapon wouldn't matter.

I walked out to the detective and Jay. I cleared my sore throat. "Hey guys."

Aerie tucked her arm under mine.

The detective leaned forward carefully. "You should have come back into the station. Timing is everything. We could have caught the perp."

"I was a little shaken and realized that after I was back here at the Soup and Scoop."

"Can you sit down and let me take a statement?" The detective was careful to give me space.

"Yes, but the guy told me he's looking for something and I bet he was the one that broke into my house."

Detective Lockheart took notes in his pint-sized notebook.

"What I'd really like to do is check my house for any more clues. I want you guys to help me do that first."

In my mind the killer obviously believed Robbie had this key he wanted. And he had something to do with Robbie's disappearance. Whoever wanted this key thought that Robbie or I had it and was willing to murder to get it.

"I'm worried about Robbie. I think he might be the next victim if we don't figure this out soon." If he wasn't dead already.

Aerie flipped the open sign, CLOSED! SEE YOU IN A BIT! on the door of the diner. She shrugged. "We have more important things to do today. One chef is missing, and the other one doesn't need the hassle of a lunch rush." She hugged me.

On the way over, Jay pulled Aerie aside. I walked a little faster to catch up with Detective Dan, giving them privacy to make amends.

Detective Lockheart turned his head in my direction but wouldn't meet my eyes. "Look, words cannot state how distressed I am that you were assaulted outside the police station. I apologize that we're not doing a better job of keeping you safe."

I didn't know what to say to him. It was one thing for me to think these thoughts and quite another for a police detective to admit them. I just nodded and was saved from the conversation by Jay raising his voice.

"You let her stay in a house that was ransacked last night?" Jay sounded really angry at Aerie.

Her voice was raised as well. "She wanted to. You are always the one telling me to let people be."

"Why wouldn't you call me?" There was a long pause and I stared straight ahead. I didn't want them to argue about me. Jay finished the sentence with a quieter tone and I had to strain to hear him. "Call me next time. Please."

Then they were talking quickly, but not loud enough for me to hear. It didn't sound like arguing anymore. It sounded as if they were working things out.

Jay shouldn't be angry at us for not telling him things were heating up. He's the one who disappeared. I mean, I accused him of murder. He could be mad about that. But we couldn't be sharing with him every little thing that happened at my house. We'd be on the phone with him twenty-four/seven if he wanted those kinds of updates. It was almost like my sister and her need to intervene on a constant basis.

Watching Aerie and Jay hash it out reminded me that I had left things badly with Darla. When this was all over and done and things had settled down, I would make it a point to call her, if only to let her know I was okay.

WE ENTERED my house as a group. Detective Lockheart methodically made his way through each room taking photos and collecting evidence.

I finally took him upstairs to show him the attic. "The night of the fire, before the fire, Aerie had been the only one up here to make sure the windows were locked.

Detective Lockheart turned to face Aerie. "Do you recall seeing footprints in the dust?"

"Not that I remember. But I was focused on locking the windows."

He took photographs of the footprints. I stood staring down at the ridges that the prints had made in the dust. They reminded me again of work boots. I snuck a look at Detective Lockheart's feet in his black dress shoes. And suddenly I flashed back to my view of the perpetrator's feet, right before I brought up my knee outside the police station. He had been wearing boots.

18

After inspecting my house, Detective Lockhart headed back to the station to analyze everything he found including the photos of the boot print in the attic.

Aerie made me swear to stay home and nurse my injuries. "They are minor Aerie. I can still help at the diner."

"I'd feel better if you stayed home and rested. Even better if you rested at Jay's and my house"

Jay nodded. Where was the guy who thought his sister was overreacting about my safety?

I nodded to let her know I understood. Maybe it was best that I stayed home. I could formulate a plan to catch this jerk. Expanding on the list of everything we knew and allowing my mind to think on it for a bit in the quiet house was something I couldn't do at the diner. Not if Aerie continued to play mama bear.

"I know you guys think I'll be safer at your house, but honestly, I really need to be in my own space to think for a while."

"You want to rest here? Give me a sec." Jay pulled out his phone and walked to the next room to make a call.

Aerie closed the gap between us and whispered, "He was really mad that we didn't tell him what was going on."

Before I could respond, Jay strode back into the room. "Okay, all set. An officer will be stationed outside of your house until things calm down. Dan agreed it was the best way to make sure you're safe. He's feeling really guilty about what happened to you at the station. It probably doesn't seem like it, but we aim to keep each other safe here."

Part of me didn't want someone watching the house all the time, but a bigger part of me felt relieved.

After I assured them that my phone was charged and that I would stay home, they left. Aerie went back to the diner; Jay went back to his work site.

Arnold jumped up on the card table I used as a dining table and I stroked his fur as I looked over the list. Each sentence represented clues and evidence.

I read through the list again. The latest one, the key, stuck in my head. What key was he looking for and why? I remembered the old key I found under the oven, but recounting the threatening conversations I had heard from Mr. Meyer, I realized maybe the key had something to do with the bank.

I had a friend at the bank. Who would probably be beyond thrilled to help me out today.

I waved to the cop sitting in her car outside my house. I only felt a little guilty that I had told Aerie and Jay that I would rest all afternoon.

I stepped over the threshold into the bank foyer. Ellie perked up. Before she could say anything, I asked in a quiet voice, "Is Mr. Meyer here?"

"No, he actually just went over to the diner for lunch." She leaned forward. "How's the puppy?"

"We named her Toto for the time being. She's fine. Hey Ellie, are there duplicates of safety deposit box keys?"

"The only copy of safety deposit box keys are the ones that Mr. Meyer holds. They are kept locked in his office."

"Someone has been threatening him, something about a key. Could it be about a copy of a safety deposit box key?"

"Maybe. I suppose if someone had lost their key or something like that they would have to talk to Mr. Meyer about it. Hey, you've heard from Robbie, right?"

"No, Detective Lockhart said they found his truck, but they haven't found him. We're getting pretty worried about him, actually. "

"Really? I thought he was back. If it wasn't him then I saw someone in his house."

"Are you sure?"

"Yeah, I figured he was back and that he had called Aerie about the dog."

I had to get Aerie and Detective Lockhart. I needed to know if Robbie was okay. "Thanks for all the information, Ellie, I really appreciate it."

"Are you going over to Robbie's house? I wish I could come with you."

"Don't worry I'll let you know what I find out. In the meantime, when Mr. Meyer gets back, can you have him call me? I need to ask him a few questions."

If Robbie was back and hadn't let any of us know then he was in some serious hot water with Aerie, but if someone else was in his house, like searching for a key, maybe we could catch them red handed.

AERIE WAS SURPRISINGLY happy to close the diner for the second time within the hour so we could check Robbie's house again. She was not happy I had been investigating without her.

"All I did was ask Ellie a few questions at the bank. Perfectly safe."

"Mira, the last time someone tried to hurt you, you were literally outside the police station."

She had me there. "Okay, so next time, I'll wait until you are off work, okay?" Her mood changed quickly once I shared Ellie's information.

"I'm cleaning and closing now. I'll drive over to your house and pick you up."

I stopped at the cruiser outside my house and asked the cop if she had radio access to Detective Lockheart. When I told her what it was about, she agreed to let me contact him over the radio. I sat in the front of her cruiser and filled in the detective on what Ellie said. He let the station know that he was heading over to Robbie's to check into a sighting at his house. The chief directed people to be on the ready, in case it wasn't Robbie himself, but someone dangerous.

I hopped out of the cruiser to quickly walk Toto and pet Arnold until Aerie showed. Jay was with her. I had thought he went to work, but he said he helped Aerie with the lunch service.

When we arrived in Robbie's neighborhood, the house was quiet. We parked behind two cruisers.

Detective Lockheart and the chief had arrived and were preparing to enter the house. The chief called out, "We're professionals. Please let us handle this situation. All of you, stay here."

They headed closer to the house quickly and

methodically. First, they knocked and yelled into the house several times without a reply. Then the detective used his window-breaking pen to pop the window out of the front door. They opened it and went inside.

After what felt like an eternity, the chief came out and walked toward the car with a grim look on his face. "It's all under control. Detective Lockheart is inside taking photographs and collecting evidence. We would like you all to go home. I'll be in touch, later.

Aerie rushed forward. "Have you found Robbie?"

The chief nodded his head. "Yes. Unfortunately, I have had to notify the coroner."

"What?" Aerie's voice came out as a gasp. Jay rushed to her side to keep her from collapsing.

"We need you all to go home," the chief announced.

Aerie began to cry. Jay took her by the arm and led her back to the car.

I stared at the chief in disbelief. I couldn't believe Robbie was dead. We were too late. My shoulders slumped and I looked down at my feet. Then I noticed the chief's feet. Or rather his boots. Boots that looked remarkably familiar. My throat constricted; I couldn't breathe.

What could I do? I was standing in front of the killer. This same man had attacked me outside the police station. The chief was the correct height. I had a hunch the tread on his boots would match the ones in my attic.

He had been arguing with Mr. Meyer. Had he been trying to get a safety deposit box key?

He also had a bandage on the side of his wrist. I wondered if a cat's scratch caused the wound.

All of this ran through my head in what felt like hours. But in reality, it was a few brief seconds. The chief couldn't see the realization in my eyes. Or at least I hoped he couldn't.

I brought a hand to my face and pretended to cry. "Okay, Chief." I headed toward the car.

"Ms. Michaels." I turned around, now a safe distance from him. "I'll need to see you back at the police station for questioning."

He didn't need me for questioning. I had the sinking feeling he wanted to get me alone again. But that was never going to happen. Yet, I had to make him think everything was fine. "Sure, Chief. I can come in whenever it's convenient for you. Obviously, you have your hands full right now."

He nodded and went back into the house.

Aerie was sobbing in the backseat. I climbed in next to her and sat. "It's the chief."

Jay's jaw dropped. "You think he's the murderer?"

"He's definitely the one who grabbed me outside the police station. Dan hasn't come back out..."

Aerie let out a gasp and looked up at the house. "You think something has happened to Dan?"

"I just find it hard to believe that regardless of what Dan found, he wouldn't come out and let us know. And that he would let the chief shoo us away."

"We have to help Dan. He can't die too." Aerie straightened up like she was going to storm the house.

Jay put his hand on the door, but he paused. "That's the chief of police in there. If we go in, he'll have to kill us all to keep the town from knowing it has been him from the start." Jay put his hand on his sister's leg to steady her.

"The best way to save Dan is to prove that the chief is the murderer, the arsonist, and the burglar." My mind raced back to my lists and index cards. I just needed one more hole filled in before I could explain everything.

"How exactly do you plan on proving the chief did all this?" Jay asked.

"We set a trap."

19

My cell phone rang.

Perfect. It was Ellie.

"Mira, I wanted to let you know that Mr. Meyer is here."

"I'll be right there." I looked at Jay and Aerie. I wanted them to be safe. And I had an idea that was anything but safe.

"I need you both to talk to Mr. Meyer. Ask him about the chief and their argument. I'll stay here and wait for you to get back."

Jay looked at the house. "If he decides to leave, there's not much you can do about it."

"I guess I can follow him."

Jay shook his head. "I'll stay. Aerie can go with you. I don't want either of you alone right now, even if I have eyes on the chief."

Kind and caring as the last twenty-four hours had shown, Jay wanted to protect us. I think I knew how I could get this to play out and have the chief confess, but before anything else happened we needed more proof. I put my hand on Aerie's. "Can you go to the bank? Talk to Mr. Meyer.

But it has to be right now. We don't have any time to waste. I will wait in Dan's car and lock the doors." I could tell that Jay wanted to get Aerie out of here. He agreed.

Aerie gripped my hand. "Swear to me you won't leave this car once you've locked the doors."

I nodded. Knowing full well I wasn't doing any of that.

I got out of the car. I hopped into the front of Dan's cruiser and waved my hand, showing them that I'd be safe.

Aerie pointed a silent finger at me. She mouthed the word, *Stay*. I nodded. Sorry Aerie, I thought, I have to do this.

As soon as the car was out of sight, I opened the door and got out. But then thought better of it and sat back in the driver's seat once again, this time pulling out the CB like the cop did at my house.

I radioed into the station. "This is Mira Michaels. I'm at 11 Walnut street." I stopped. What would I say to the police that they would believe?

"Where is Detective Lockheart?"

"Something has happened to him. Send someone right away." It was the truth. At least, I thought so. Something had to have happened to Dan or he would have come out here himself to tell Aerie about Robbie.

Before they could ask me any more questions, I put the CB back and got out of the car, letting the door close quietly. I wanted the chief to think I had left with Aerie and Jay.

I crouched and made my way to the side of the house. If I was very careful, I could try to look inside. I inched closer to the window. I reached out and put my fingers on the sill and pulled myself ever so slightly up and looked into the window. A pair of surprised eyes met mine.

Shocked, I dropped to the ground. He had seen me. I bit my lip. I didn't have Dan's car keys. Before I could get up to run, a viselike grip closed around my shoulder and yanked me up. "What are you still doing here?" the chief spit in my face.

"I wanted to see what was going on?" Could I play dumb? But one look into the chief's eyes and I knew I wouldn't get away with it.

"You're coming with me." He pushed me in front of him and I could feel the cold hard prod of a metal barrel in my right kidney. A million thoughts raced through my head but only one that mattered. I had to keep the chief talking until the police showed up.

He shoved me over the threshold into the house where both Robbie and Dan were gagged and tied to kitchen chairs. Robbie tried to get up, but the chair held him back. Dan was out cold. Thank goodness they were alive. All the more reason to keep the chief talking.

"Why did you kill Becca?"

"None of your business." He grabbed the third kitchen chair and shoved me into it. "You're just an insignificant outsider. You don't belong here, and you don't deserve the house."

"What is it about that house?" I legitimately wanted to know.

"The house is supposed to be mine. Along with everything inside of it." The chief was out of rope and grabbed a dishtowel to knot my hands to the chair. The towel wasn't long enough to tie both my hands, but he did manage to cut off the circulation on one wrist as he tied it to the back of the chair. I tugged at it. "You're not going to get away with this. Everyone already knows."

"Because of you." He pointed the gun at my face.

I cringed by reflex.

"What are you going to do, kill all three of us?" I

shouted, and suddenly regretted putting the idea in his head.

He looked confused. He wasn't sure what to do. "That house is supposed to be mine. Not yours. You and all your meddling. That fire was supposed to shut you up. A lot of good it did."

Where were the police? What was taking them so long? I should've called the fire department, they seem to show up pretty quickly for all my other gigantic mistakes.

Where were they? The kitchen was stuffy and a bead of sweat trickled down the side of my face. I was determined to talk my way out of this, if at all possible.

"Why do you deserve the house?" I yanked again at the dish towel. It seemed to tighten even more.

"Because my mother owned it before you. It should be mine, not yours. I want the chest."

"But why kill Becca?" I watched as he continued to search the drawers for something.

"That was an accident. She refused to give me the key to the chest...kept telling me she didn't have it, and things got out of hand." The chief found what he was looking for and stuffed a cloth napkin into my mouth.

I struggled to keep him from doing it, but it was futile. I tried to kick his shins and got in a good one, but the others ended up kicking Dan's chair. Dan's head lolled to the side. As much as he annoyed me, I hoped he wasn't dead.

The chief paced up and down the kitchen. I really wondered what he planned to do. And then he began talking to himself. I just hoped he wouldn't talk himself into killing the three of us.

"Mother should have given me the house. None of this had to happen."

The front door slammed. Chief Orsa spun around.

"Beau! Beau Theodore Orsa!" An old lady shouted into the house. I recognized the yell of an irate mother. Mrs. Orsa? I shook my head. Where are the police? A car door slammed out front.

Mrs. Orsa marched into the kitchen. The chief stood stock still with a very confused look on his face. "Mom? What are you doing here?" The wrist of his hand in which he held the gun went limp.

"I'm hearing that you've done some very bad things." She pushed past him to stand in between me and the chief. I managed to push the cloth out of my mouth.

"Mira!" Aerie stopped short at the entrance into the kitchen. "Robbie!"

The chief pointed his gun in Aerie's direction and Jay pushed her behind him.

Mrs. Orsa glared at her son. "Why do you have that gun out? Put that down. NOT in your holster. Onto the table!"

Chief Orsa reluctantly put his gun on the kitchen table. And stared astonished at his mother. "All I wanted was the chest and the key, Mother. It's supposed to be mine."

"For years you stared at that chest thinking it was full of treasure. And look where it got you. You don't deserve the key *or* the house," she snapped.

Aerie walked behind Detective Lockheart. She untied his bindings and then she loosened mine. I rubbed my hand as pins and needles shot up my arm. But I kept one eye on that gun on the kitchen table just in case Chief Orsa changed his mind.

Aerie untied Robbie and gave him a quick hug.

"Now wait a minute." Chief Orsa pushed forward.

Jay scooped the gun off the table, checked the safety, and stuck it in his back pocket. A glance at the look in his eye told me if anything went south, he would be ready to throw some punches, or use the gun, if need be.

"You wait a minute, Beau. You've gone too far. I won't let this go on anymore." The little old lady took the chief by his large muscular arm and tugged him toward the chair that Robbie had just vacated. "You sit right down here. You give me those handcuffs." She pointed at them and the chief did as his mother said. Surprisingly, he allowed her to handcuff him to the chair.

"Mother, I can explain."

"Did you have anything to do with Becca? That poor girl."

"It was an accident." He looked pleadingly at his mother.

Mrs. Orsa's rock-hard façade cracked, and her eyes welled up. "I raised you better than this." She sniffled. "You were always my little bear. Look at what you've done. I'm ashamed of you."

Chief Orsa slouched, his arms cuffed behind his back.

Mrs. Orsa then let out a deep breath and collapsed into a nearby chair. She put her face in her hands and sobbed quietly. I poured a glass of water for her from the kitchen sink and placed it on the table next to her. She sipped, her eyes never making contact with her son again.

Two police officers entered the kitchen from behind Jay. "What is going on here?"

I poured a glass of water from the tap and sprinkled it on Dan's face. He flinched and came to rather quickly.

"What? The chief..." He jerked and almost fell out of the chair.

"Relax. Everything is under control. I just need you to wake up and explain what happened so they can take chief Orsa into custody."

He glanced at the chief and back at me. "I told you to leave the investigating to me."

"I'll remember that for next time." I grinned.

Detective Lockheart stood, rubbed the back of his head, and recited the Miranda warning to the chief. When he finished, he unlocked the cuffs and pulled the chief out of the chair, and handed him over to the police.

"Chief, I believe you have a cell at the station waiting for you."

The chief spat out, "None of this would have happened, Mother, if you had just given me the key. And the house."

Dan followed the police with the chief outside. And as we followed, Robbie stopped me and put his hand on my shoulder. "Thanks, Mira."

"Why did the chief think you'd have the key that he wants?"

"Becca was my girlfriend; the chief thought she had given me the key once we got it from Mrs. Orsa's safe deposit box."

Mrs. Orsa said nothing as we drove her home. She disappeared into her house and closed the door.

20

Detective Lockheart placed Orsa in jail. He called the coroner in the city and found out that Orsa had never sent Becca's body for an autopsy. He now understood why the evidence continually went missing. Orsa had access to all of it and made sure that no one could piece together that he had anything to do with the murder or the fire that helped destroy any additional evidence. Still, Detective Lockheart reminded me to leave the detective work to the professionals. When I mentioned I had DNA from the cat scratching him when he broke into my house, detective Lockheart almost lost it.

"That was verifiable evidence and because you took it from the veterinary office, there's no way it can be entered as proper evidence for this case."

"You can't use it at all?"

"I'll say it again, leave the investigative work to the professionals."

As much as I wanted to I didn't remind him that one of those professionals was the perpetrator of everything that happened over the last week, but I was certain if I bothered to mention it he'd probably shoot laser beams out of his eyes.

Once things settled down, Robbie, Aerie, and I gathered at the diner.

I handed Toto, whose real name was Ozzy, to Robbie and she nestled into his neck. Aerie and I smiled. "I can't believe that Orsa held you at your own house for days."

Robbie frowned. "It drove Ozzy crazy. Orsa kept me gagged and hidden in the basement while he was trying to get information out of me. I was afraid he was going to do something to Ozzy to try to make me talk. I was so relieved when you guys came around and got her."

He turned to Aerie. "Sorry, Aerie, I need to leave town. Becca's death has been hard. I plan to take her dad into the city and see if I can get him back into treatment. He's pretty broken up over her death. I haven't seen my family in a while and, well, it's a place to start. I can't say when or if I'll be back." With Ozzy still in his arms, he hugged Aerie for a long moment and then gave me a quick hug. "See you guys around. Mira, will you keep Ozzy for me? I can't take her with me."

"Are you sure?" He handed the dog to me and she licked my face.

"She's taken to you and I don't know what my situation will be going forward." His grin was a sad one.

Aerie smiled through her tears. After all, it was just hours ago that we thought he had joined Becca. "Do what you need to do. Your job will be waiting for you here. We'll really miss you, especially the customers. You're the best chef."

"And that's no lie. I've done that job. It's not easy," I said.

"I heard you did a decent job while I was gone."

"Only if you count my ability to create events for the fire department." We laughed together.

"Thank you, guys, again, for rescuing Ozzy and me. Without you I don't know what would've happened. The chief was desperate to get hold of that key. You never found it, huh?"

I remembered the key that I found in the kitchen when Jay and I had been cleaning up. "I'll be right back." I ran home and stopped for a moment to look up at the eaves and the slate roof and wondered just how many secrets this house held. I unlocked the door and stepped inside. The house felt different: no longer tense and guarded. I made my way down to the basement and leaned over the front of the washer to retrieve the key I had placed on the shelf a week ago. The cool brass slowly warmed in my hand. "So, you're the key that has been causing all these problems." I wrapped my fingers around it and made my way back to the Soup and Scoop.

I opened my hand in front of Robbie. "I found this under the old oven after the kitchen fire. Is this the kind of key you're talking about?"

Robbie reached out to pick it up. He rolled it between his fingers. "This is it." He turned it and let the light shine on the decorative head of the key. "Under the oven you said?"

I nodded.

"Becca must have dropped it or kicked it under there when she was threatened by Orsa."

"In a way, the chief setting fire to the house actually helped us find it."

"Why would someone want something so bad they'd be willing to kill for it?"

"Desperate people." Robbie handed the key back to me. "I'm heading out."

After many goodbyes and farewells, Robbie drove off. Aerie and I stood outside my house.

Before anything else, I knew I needed to call Darla. Aerie said she'd wait for me on the front stoop while I walked into the backyard.

"Hey, Darla. It's me."

"Are you okay?"

"Yep, why wouldn't I be?" I announced cheerfully.

"Oh, no reason." But I could hear it in her voice. She had seen something.

"I'm fine. No worries. The house is going to work out. And I have even made a new friend; her name is Aerie."

"That's wonderful. Mira, I really want to talk but I'm running late for my next reading."

"No, problem. I just wanted to let you know it's all good here and I'm fine."

"Mira. Keep in touch okay?"

"Sure. Have a good reading."

"I'll call you."

I smiled at the phone and ended the call. I knew she would.

I walked around to the front of the house and stood next to Aerie. We looked up at the peak of the roof, the area that made the attic look like a cathedral. I turned the key over in my hand. "Should we see where it fits?"

"Every key has a lock."

We made our way to the base of the attic steps.

The attic now had a warm glow to it, but it still held its secrets.

The dark wooden chest sat where it had probably sat for a century.

The back wall was lit by the single light bulb and I marveled at the dark wood and the bright brass lock plate that gleamed in the dim light.

"So, this key..." I rolled it in my hand... "fits in that lock. We're about to find out what kind of treasure it really holds." I kneeled next to the chest.

"This is exciting." Aerie joined me.

The head of the key had a beautiful curved shape. The shape was mirrored in the plate on the front of the chest.

I lined up the end of the key to the lock and slowly inserted it. I twisted it clockwise. A low click sounded as the drum turned and released the lock. Letting go of the key, I was able to push the lid open.

Inside the chest sat a stack of newspapers and another large wooden box.

Aerie reached in and, with my help, we pulled the box from the chest. "This is what Chief Orsa killed for?"

I ran my hand along the top. "No. He was willing to kill for the possibilities."

Aerie leaned forward. "Are you going to open it?"

We pried open the wooden lid and found it full of tiny bottles. It was a 19th century apothecary box.

"It's beautiful." I stared at the dark wood and the gleaming glass bottles.

A wistful voice said, *It's mine.*

I turned to Aerie. "What did you say?"

"I agreed, it is beautiful."

"I thought you said it was yours?" A cold chill ran up my spine. I realized it hadn't been Aerie's voice. I wasn't letting the thought of a ghost in the house even enter my thoughts.

"It's obviously yours now, it's in your attic." She grinned.

"It's so sad that Becca had to die for this. Mrs. Orsa kept saying it was priceless and held the history of the house. But

I don't think that this is what Orsa thought his mom meant, do you? Newspapers and an apothecary set?

"I doubt it." Aerie shifted anxiously.

Had she heard the ghost? I didn't think she had.

She turned to me. "Will you work with me at the Soup and Scoop?"

"What?" The change in subject confused me.

"I know Jay isn't interested in cooking, with his construction company and everything." With a wave she dismissed the unspoken idea that he was still dating Chelsea. But I knew what she meant.

"You know, you don't actually have to ask me. I love working there."

"It'll take time away from renovating your house."

"It means I can make some cash so I can actually fix up the place. So, you're doing me a favor."

"Maybe I can get Chelsea to break up with Jay and then you and Jay can get together."

"I highly doubt Jay would want to date me. I did accuse him of murder."

"Well, you feel like a sister to me and I want to keep it that way."

"You got it, sis. So what soup are we cooking for lunch this week?"

"Maybe we should try the chicken corn soup again?"

"As long as I don't burn down the diner."

"That's what sprinkler systems are for." She made her way down the attic steps.

I followed her, and then I stopped and looked back at the apothecary box. It was getting harder and harder to deny that I might not be alone in this house.

If I ignored it long enough maybe this whole ghost thing would go away.

But I was curious about this house and its secrets. I planned to start with the old newspapers and see what history they held.

Aerie stopped at the bottom of the attic stairs. Her grip tightened on the banister. She turned to face me, her face pale and anxious. "Mira, I have that bad feeling again."

"Maybe your vibes are telling us not to make the soup."

She forced a slight grin. "Maybe you're right." She hesitated before she turned around and continued down the stairs.

"Whatever it is, I'm sure we can solve it." After this past week I was sure nothing could get in our way.

Because Clara and I will help. Arnold purred as he wove around my shins.

I was afraid he'd say something like that. I could only hope we wouldn't have the need to solve any more mysteries. But then who was I kidding?

PREVIEW OF PRANKS AND POISON

The onions were beginning to burn again. The house already smelled like scorched vegetables. The trash can was filled with them. Arnold had abandoned me for the other room. Even Ozzy my friendly foster dog was no where to be found, her sensitive nose had lost patience as well. I couldn't seem to figure out the sauté function on this electric pressure cooker.

If I had a regular stove this wouldn't be happening, but I ignored the burned-out hole that had been my kitchen. Doing that allowed me to ignore the memory of finding the body of my realtor on my first day in town and the memory of the night of the fire when Arnold and the resident ghost, Clara, helped me get out in time.

I stirred the onions and prodded the sauté button again. Oh, it worked. The pot stopped smoking and settled into a sizzle.

I rummaged through the grocery bags I had recently brought in and found the treats I had bought for both my companions. "Hey, guys, I've got treats for you." Nothing happened. I shook the box of dog treats and the bag of kitty treats. A mini stampede of animals arrived. Ozzy bounced her fuzzy brown terrier body which was smaller than the regal black long fur or Arnold who sat expectantly with golden eyes glowing.

"There's no help for it guys, I'm going to have to use this front room as a kitchen until the construction is done." Ozzy bounded off with her treat. She was so friendly and content to play by herself with her toys. Which helped me feel better because I was at the diner so much these days.

In humorous contrast, Arnold sat there expectantly. "Do you want a treat, buddy?" I pulled out two of them and put them on the floor for him. I knew better than to ask him to do something, like beg for the treat. He'd likely suffocate me in my sleep with his furry body if I did that.

I washed the treat dust off my hands in the small bathroom under the stairs and went back to my onions. The beginnings of a soup I hoped to perfect for the diner. I loved working for Aerie at the Soup and Scoop as a cook, which I was extremely grateful for. I desperately needed the money to fix the kitchen and get back to flipping this house. My plan was to move on to the next big flip. So I could finally show my sister that I could be independent. Truly independent without receiving constant input from my big sister.

As if on cue, my cell phone rang. I stopped stirring the onions and closed my eyes. It would not surprise me in the least if it was her.

I reached in my pocket and pulled out the phone. Sure enough, my sister's somber, meditative face stared at me from my cell phone, her name in bold at the top of the screen: Darla Damian. It was her "stage" name. Her nom de plume, her fake front. I sighed. She wasn't a fake, I had to admit. She was a real-deal psychic, and she made her fortune doing it. I just wished she'd leave me out of it. I wanted nothing to do with the family "inheritance." She swore I had the gift too, but I don't. Well, except for hearing my cat's voice in my mind telling me important things like the discount cat food I dared to buy him was stale or the heating mat in his kitty bed needed to be turned on. As if on cue, Arnold chimed in. *Why won't you answer Darla?*

I remembered Arnold told me I sighed audibly whenever Darla called, so he always knew. I ignored the call, letting it roll to voicemail. "I don't need Darla telling me all the reasons I shouldn't have moved here." She had micromanaged me since we were kids. Having a sister who could sense the future and truly knew it was annoying on so many levels.

Immediately the phone rang again. I seriously contemplated blocking her calls, but this time it wasn't her number on the phone screen. It was an unknown number.

"Hello?"

"Is this Mira Michaels?"

"Yes."

"This is Elaine Dunbar, from the cat show. You rescued Oksana for me."

"Oh, hi. How are you and how's Oksana?"

"That's what I'd like to talk to you about. Thank you again for saving Oksana. I don't really know how to tell you this, but we have a situation."

Elaine explained the situation in far more detail than necessary. All the while I marched through the house to hunt down Arnold. Just as I was ending the call, I backtracked and found him lying innocently in a dollop of sunshine, near the porch window.

"You've got some explaining to do."

Hmm? *I'm napping.* His fluffy black fur barely moved.

"I just got a call asking me to go 50-50 on vet bills for your little friend Oksana."

His head snapped toward me. Was she injured?

"No, you naughty cat, she's going to have kittens! And you're responsible."

Really? That's wonderful news. He relaxed into the sunshine.

"Do you know how many mouths to feed that is?"

Doesn't the mother feed them?

"Ooh, Arnold you are on my last nerve. How could you do this?"

I could have sworn he grinned. It was easy.

I shook my head and forced myself to do some deep breathing exercises that Aerie taught in her yoga classes. Breathe in. Breathe out. Not much I could do about kittens. Or paying for future vet bills. I sighed and went back to my soup before I burned another batch of onions.

EARLY MONDAY MORNING at the diner had its own flow, and Aerie and I had just begun when my cell phone rang. My sister, again. I had lost count of how many times she called yesterday. She was nothing if not persistent. I turned the phone's ringer off and stuffed it back into my pocket. She wasn't going to stop calling until I answered. I wasn't in the mood for her brand of lecture.

Aerie looked up from the computer at the cash register, her blond hair pulled back in a snug ponytail. "Who are you ignoring?"

"Ignoring? Oh, it's my sister."

I shrugged it off. I needed to start a new soup recipe and I was really worried about how it would taste.

"Siblings are important. Maybe she needs something."

If anyone knew about how annoying siblings could be, it was Aerie. Her brother, Jay, was dating the girl who bullied Aerie all through middle school. Definite conflict there. "She doesn't need anything. She never needs anything from me. Except to give me a lecture. And I need to focus on our new soup this morning."

Aerie shrugged. "Okay, but you know your sister is with you your whole life. You should find ways to make your relationship work for each other."

I raised an eyebrow. "Are you taking up psychology?"

"Meditation gives me insight." She stretched her arms and smiled. "What soup are you making today?"

"Hungarian mushroom." I took a deep breath. "I made a small batch at home and it tasted really good. But I don't know if I can increase the amount for the diner and have it still be tasty."

"I have faith in you. You can do it."

"Thanks, Mama Duck."

"Mama Duck?"

"You know that little picture book about Quack the duck who's afraid to swim?" I couldn't help but smile at the recollection of my own mother reading it to me and Darla. "She tells him she has faith that he can do it. And he does."

"I will happily be your Mama Duck."

"Thanks." I grabbed an apron off the hook and walked into the refrigerator. This soup would taste great. I hoped. I filled Aerie in on Arnold's antics and the kitten fiasco, while we got ready for the breakfast rush. "I love kittens. Will the owner let you keep one, do you think?"

"That's the least of my worries at this point. I need to figure out how to pay the vet bills until the glorious day." I went back to focusing on my prep work.

I had to admit I was getting better at cooking over-easy eggs and keeping the bacon grease from burning down the diner. I still hadn't mastered pancake pouring but at least I wasn't undercooking them anymore. And now I understood why toast was always served cold in restaurants. You could never time it properly in order to have the toast pop by the time the egg was done on the grill. At least I could stick it under the heat lamp while I finished cooking the egg.

I was getting to like small-town living. I knew almost everyone's name who came in and they now knew me. Of course, the murder in my house had mostly helped with my celebrity.

Mr. Meyer smiled and held up the toast with his melted butter on it. He appreciated the effort. He also appreciated that I helped put Sheriff Orsa behind bars and he was no longer harassing Mr. Meyer at work at the bank.

Aside from a few patrons like Mr. Meyer, the Monday breakfast rush had been mostly to-go coffee-drinkers. It let me get ready for the real rush, everyone came in for lunch.

Aerie finished bussing the dining room while I started prepping the mushroom soup. I propped my phone up on the shelf above the stove and read the recipe, careful to make sure my phone was on vibrate. Maybe I should just block Darla's calls altogether, maybe for just a little while.

First step: chop and sauté onions. Easy enough. I planned to quadruple the recipe. I did the math in my head and grabbed four large, sweet onions. I halved and peeled them and began chopping. We had started using sweet onions last week when we realized I didn't cry as much while I chopped them. It made me a little antsy to be bleary-eyed while handling a sharp knife near my fingers. Switching to sweet onions also seemed to make everything taste better.

I turned on the burner and listened to the gas pop as it lit under the large soup pot on the stove. I drizzled in the extra-virgin olive oil and allowed it to heat up.

My knife skills were not professional. It took me a while to chop up the onions, but it was extremely satisfying to hear them sizzle when I dropped them into the hot oil.

I stirred them briefly with the long bamboo spoon. Then I headed to the walk-in refrigerator for the mushrooms. I had four pounds of cremini mushrooms to chop. And a handful of dry mushrooms that would need to soak. The dry mushrooms were easy enough. I just poured hot water from the percolator over them in a dish. They would have to sit and wait until they softened enough for me to chop them. But I looked down at the four large containers of mushrooms. They were covered in soil. Rinsing them wasn't going to be quick.

I grabbed the largest colander from one of the bottom shelves and took it over to the sink. I could only dump one container of mushrooms at a time into the colander. I turned the sprayer on and realized I had to rub each and every mushroom until it was clean. I definitely did not want grit to ruin my soup.

I let out a huge sigh as I washed the final batch of mushrooms. I now had a huge counter full of clean mushrooms to chop. I glanced up at the clock--already 11:15. Where had the time gone?

"Aerie! I need help with the mushrooms."

I didn't hear anything from the dining room. I dried off my hands and walked out to the counter. The room was completely empty. "Where did she go?" If I wanted to get the soup ready for lunch, I couldn't look for her. I sent her a quick text and then got back to the kitchen.

I needed to chop fast. While keeping all my fingers.

After trying to pin the mushrooms down at an angle and slice them quickly, I decided to pull off all the stems and set them aside. That way I could lay the caps flat on the cutting board and chop them in rows. It seemed to be a more efficient way to chop everything, but it still took time. If today was like a normal Monday, customers would start to arrive around 11:30.

As the board filled with chopped mushrooms, I threw them into the pot and stirred with the bamboo spoon.

I had to watch the heat of the pot. I couldn't risk burning the onions. I added some water and continued chopping.

My mind wandered. It wasn't like Aerie to take off and leave me to fend for myself. She knew I wasn't adept yet in the kitchen and often needed another set of hands. Where was she and why hadn't she let me know she was leaving? This was not like her.

MORE MIRA MICHAELS MYSTERIES

If you enjoyed this story and would like to read more about Mira and her lovable cat Arnold, check out more of the Mira Michaels Mysteries.

Keys and Catastrophes
Pranks and Poison
Construction and Calamity

Please consider writing a review on Amazon to let others know more about Mira's adventures, please don't share spoilers! Reviews help readers find these stories which helps writers like me. That way I can continue to write what I love and create more stories for you.

Thanks bunches,

Julia

THANK YOU

A book is a mighty undertaking, and I could not have done it without the help of some very key individuals. Thank you, Heather Gerry Kelly, because without your cheerleading and excellent editing skills I would have lost my nerve. You keep me motivated and supported and I simply cannot put it into words how much that means to me. Thank you for believing with me, that all writers deserve to be heard.

Thank you to Cindy Davis for her editing help. I will continue to work on my excessive use of split modifiers.

Thank you to Susan Kaye Quinn who, in so many ways, showed me how to create a business out of something I love.

Thank you to my daughter for brainstorming with me throughout the entire process.

Thank you to Mr. Peat, my high school English teacher, who encouraged me to write.

Thank you to the indie publishing community for their unerring support of me and fellow writers. Together we are creating a new world of stories.

SUBSCRIBE AND SAVE!

Simply go to Julia's website at www.juliakoty.com and click the subscribe button. You'll be included in our exclusive club and be the first to learn about new releases and special deals on the stories you love.

And if you haven't already read Cats and Catnapping, you'll receive it FREE when you sign up.

ABOUT THE AUTHOR

Julia Koty is an emerging author of cozy mysteries. This is the second book in the Mira Michaels Mysteries.

Julia spent her early childhood in a small town in Pennsylvania very similar to Pleasant Pond. Her house, also an old Victorian which her dad renovated, was indeed haunted.

Visit her website and subscribe to her newsletter to be a part of the group and learn about exclusive deals on upcoming books in the series.

 facebook.com/JuliaKotyAuthor